FROM THE
NANCY DREW FILES

THE CASE: Nancy tries to keep Hal Taylor on the air
and out of harm's way.

CONTACT: News producer Otto Liski produces a
winner in Taylor's corner . . . Nancy Drew.

SUSPECTS: Marilyn Morgan—the co-anchor of the
evening news, she has never forgiven Taylor for
breaking off their off-camera relationship.

Gary Krieger—a beat reporter who believes he does
all the work while Taylor takes all the credit.

Steve Gilbert—a local politician who's the subject
of Taylor's report on corruption in high places . . .
and he'll do anything to kill the story.

COMPLICATIONS: Hal Taylor is as gorgeous and
charming as they come, and he's working those
charms on Nancy. Will she change channels, choos-
ing Hal and leaving Ned in the dark? Stay tuned.

Books in The Nancy Drew Files® Series

Available from ARCHWAY Paperbacks

The Nancy Drew Files™

Case 78
Update On Crime
Carolyn Keene

AN ARCHWAY PAPERBACK
Published by POCKET BOOKS
New York   London   Toronto   Sydney   Tokyo   Singapore

AN ARCHWAY PAPERBACK *Original*

An Archway Paperback published by
POCKET BOOKS, a division of Simon & Schuster Inc.
1230 Avenue of the Americas, New York, NY 10020

ISBN: 0-671-73082-7

First Archway Paperback printing December 1992

10 9 8 7 6 5 4 3 2 1

Cover art by Tricia Zimic

Printed in the U.S.A.

IL 6+

Update On Crime

Chapter
One

NANCY, I can't believe it! That outfit makes you look just like a real anchorwoman!" Bess Marvin said, staring at Nancy Drew's reflection in the dressing room mirror.

"You think it's okay?" Nancy asked. She turned to get a better view of the jewel-toned suit she was trying on. It was a lot more formal than the clothes she usually wore. The sapphire woolen jacket and skirt matched her eyes and contrasted beautifully with her strawberry blond hair. The cream-colored silk blouse complemented her rosy complexion.

"Definitely," Bess said, nodding decisively. "I can't believe you're heading off to a glamorous

TV job, while I'm stuck flipping burgers in this ugly thing," she added, smoothing a candy-striped ruffle on her pink-and-brown skirt. "These horizontal stripes must make me look at least five pounds heavier. If I didn't have to earn some money for the holidays, I wouldn't be caught dead wearing a nightmare uniform like this."

Nancy had picked up Bess from her waitressing job at a café in their hometown of River Heights. Bess hadn't had time to change out of her uniform before they headed to the stores in the mall, where they were now.

"You look great in anything, Bess," Nancy said. "Besides, I'll be working at Channel Nine to solve a mystery, not to soak up the glamour."

"And you'll get to work with that handsome anchorman, Hal Taylor." Bess sighed. "Now, there's a guy I could flip burgers for! He's got those incredible dimples and that cute little cleft in his chin—m-m-mm!"

"I guess his kind of glamour won't be too hard to take," Nancy laughingly admitted as she changed out of the suit and reached for her jeans.

"George is going to die when she hears you're working there," Bess added.

George Fayne, Bess's cousin and polar opposite, was in California for a tennis tournament. Whereas George was dark-haired and athletic, Bess was fair and petite and preferred shopping to swimming any day of the week. But both girls were fans of the handsome anchorman.

"Anyway, you have to promise to introduce me

to Hal Taylor," Bess continued. "But not when I'm wearing polyester. Who knows, maybe sparks will fly."

"I promise," Nancy agreed. "There's only one problem, though. You seem to have forgotten that Hal and his co-anchor, Marilyn Morgan, are a major romantic item." On camera and off, the Channel 9 anchor team of Hal Taylor and Marilyn Morgan were the most famous couple in River Heights.

"Items can be exchanged, can't they?" Bess said mischievously, arching a blond eyebrow.

Nancy laughed as she pulled on her V-neck sweater. "You're hopeless, Bess," she teased.

The two girls gathered up the clothes Nancy had selected. Silk blouses, navy blazer, beige skirt—all the outfits were standard working gear for a television reporter.

"It almost seems silly to buy this stuff," Nancy said, "since my cover at the station is only as a reporter-trainee on their special training program. I certainly won't be going on the air."

Bess hung a rejected skirt back on its hanger, then turned to Nancy. "So did the guy from the station tell you what exactly the big mystery *is* at WRVH-TV?" Those were the call letters of Channel 9. "What was his name again?"

"Otto Liski, the news producer," Nancy replied. "He's a friend of my dad. I haven't found out the whole story yet, but it sounds like it could be serious. Evidently someone is trying to drive Hal Taylor off the air. He's been receiving threatening notes, phone calls, that sort of thing."

3

"I can't believe that someone would try to harm Hal," Bess said.

Nancy shrugged. "When Dad heard that Hal was in trouble, he suggested that they contact me. Mr. Liski's going to fill me in on what's been happening at the station when I arrive for my first day of work tomorrow."

Bess looked worried as they left the dressing room and walked to the department store cash register. "Just be careful, Nan, okay? This assignment sounds like it could be dangerous for you as well as for Hal."

"It wouldn't be the first time, but so far nothing really terrible has happened," Nancy reassured Bess as she handed her charge card to the saleswoman. "I just have to find out who's behind the threats before he—or she—does something really dangerous."

At eighteen, Nancy already had dozens of successful cases under her belt. Her crime-busting skills had made her famous as an amateur sleuth.

"Let's get going," Nancy said, gathering her shopping bags. "If we hurry we might be able to catch the beginning of the six o'clock news."

Twenty minutes later the two friends raced up the steps to Nancy's house. Just as they reached the front door, it opened, and the Drews' housekeeper, Hannah Gruen, walked out.

"Lasagna's in the microwave, Nancy," Hannah said, smiling at the girls. "I'm on my way to play bingo at the church." She pointed to a green feathered cap on her head. "See? I'm wearing my lucky hat!"

"Hope you win this time, Hannah," Nancy said, smiling fondly at the older woman. The cheerful, bustling housekeeper was more like a member of the family than an employee. She had lived with Nancy and her father, Carson Drew, ever since Nancy's mother passed away, when Nancy was very young.

Inside the house, Nancy clicked on the hall light. Out of habit she looked toward her father's book-lined study. Then she remembered that he had been called away unexpectedly on an over-night business trip. The girls headed for the kitchen.

"Ooh, lasagna." Bess peered through the glass door of the microwave. "I really shouldn't, but it looks so good. And *so* fattening."

"Haven't you ever heard of the lasagna diet, Bess?" Nancy joked, popping open a can of soda. "You lose five pounds the first week."

"Don't I wish." Her friend sighed. Bess worried constantly about her weight, even though her petite, curvy figure looked perfect to everyone else.

Nancy set the microwave's timer, and soon the spicy aroma of tomato sauce was wafting through the house. She quickly tossed a green salad, while Bess assembled the dinner trays and utensils. A few minutes later, the two girls carried their trays into the living room and set them down on the coffee table in front of the Drews' couch.

Nancy clicked on the television set with the remote control. In a second, the sleek, modern anchor desk of the Channel 9 news studio filled the screen. Chisel-jawed Hal Taylor and co-anchor Marilyn Morgan sat side by side at the anchor desk. At the far corner of the desk sat sports reporter Mike Murphy, wearing one of the brightly colored ties he was known for. Off to one side was a large weather map that was covered with tiny clouds and suns, indicating the area's weather pattern.

Hal Taylor wore an elegantly tailored charcoal suit. Marilyn Morgan wore a dark purple suit, with a gold pin and gold earrings that accentuated her blond hair. Hal Taylor led off the newscast.

"Good evening, I'm Hal Taylor. Here's what's happening in the news today. . . ." he began in his deep, baritone voice.

"Just think, Nancy," Bess said, her eyes on the TV screen. "Tomorrow you'll be working with him."

Nancy wasn't star-struck by nature, but suddenly she found her heart skipping a beat at the thought of working with the strikingly handsome anchorman. Not that she would forget about her longtime boyfriend, Ned Nickerson, she reminded herself sternly.

Just the thought of Ned's broad shoulders and warm brown eyes brought a softness to Nancy's eyes. She felt a tingle go up her spine as she remembered the last time she had visited Ned at Emerson College, where he was a student. His powerful arms had wrapped around her waist, and when he kissed her . . .

Better get back to business, Nancy thought. She forced herself to concentrate on the news broadcast.

When Hal and Marilyn weren't introducing news stories, they kept up a steady stream of chitchat. Nancy winced when they switched directly from a murder story to the station's smiling weatherman, who told a lame joke.

"I guess that's why they call it 'happy talk' news," Nancy commented, shaking her head.

" 'Stupid talk' would be more like it," Bess replied indignantly. "I never realized how ridiculous they sound sometimes." She took a bite of salad. "Anyway, happy talk doesn't seem to suit Hal tonight," she observed. "He looks kind of uncomfortable, don't you think? I've never seen him act that way before."

Bess was right. Underneath the slick surface of the broadcast, Nancy detected a current of tension. Marilyn was sitting stiff as a statue, and Hal definitely looked ill at ease. Between news stories, he kept looking off to the side, as if he expected to see someone lurking there.

Nancy leaned forward alertly. "Do you think Hal received another warning this afternoon?" she asked.

"Beats me," said Bess. She turned briefly from the screen to look at Nancy. "Why do you suppose they haven't announced anything directly about the death threats?" she wondered aloud. "Isn't that newsworthy?"

"The station managers want to keep the situation quiet so people won't know how vulnerable Hal is," Nancy told her. "That's why they haven't even called in the police yet. I wonder if—"

Suddenly Nancy and Bess heard a loud crash coming from somewhere inside the news studio. Hal Taylor's expression seemed to freeze with fear.

"What's happening to Hal?" Bess cried anxiously. As they watched, Hal stumbled over the words he was reading. Then the television screen went completely black!

Chapter

Two

AN INSTANT AFTER Hal's image disappeared, a message flashed onto the television screen: "Stand by, please. The station is experiencing technical difficulties."

"What do you think happened, Nan?" Bess asked. "Hal looked really scared just before the picture zapped out."

"I'm not sure, but I'll bet that crash we heard was a lot more than 'technical difficulties,'" Nancy said, feeling a bubble of unease. She grabbed her address book and reached for the phone that was on an end table next to the couch. "Maybe I can find out what happened by calling the station."

On her first try, Nancy got a busy signal. She was about to dial again when the news program reappeared on the screen. This time Marilyn Morgan was sitting by herself at the anchor desk. Hal was nowhere to be seen!

Marilyn apologized for the interruption, an icy expression frozen onto her attractive features. She explained that Hal had been called away to cover a breaking news story and that he would return to anchor the eleven o'clock news.

"She's certainly putting on a smooth performance," Nancy said to Bess. "But I'm not buying her explanation."

"You're right, Nancy," Bess agreed. "Hal looked white as a sheet before he disappeared— obviously *something* happened to him."

Marilyn's composure was absolute as she continued with the newscast. Nancy wondered how the woman could stay so frosty-cool under the circumstances.

Reaching for the phone again, Nancy quickly dialed another telephone number for the station that Otto Liski had given her. It took several minutes for him to come to the phone— obviously things were hectic behind the scenes at the station. When he finally came on the line, he sounded harried.

"Nancy—I'm glad you called," Liski said distractedly. "Hal's okay, but we had to cut the broadcast signal because someone slipped in a weird tape that almost got on the air."

"Weird?" Nancy echoed. "In what way?"

"It was a tape of someone in disguise threatening Hal's life," Liski said. "It kind of shook him up, so he left for the night."

"I'll be right over," Nancy said quickly.

"It can wait until tomorrow," Liski told her. "I've locked the tape up. Besides, if you came over without explanation, the staff here might not buy the intern cover we've arranged for you."

Mr. Liski was right, Nancy realized. After thanking the producer for his information, she hung up the phone.

"What happened to Hal?" Bess asked anxiously.

"He's okay," Nancy reassured her. "They had to cut the broadcast to prevent some kind of threatening tape from being aired. I'll have to wait until tomorrow to find out the details."

"Call me at the restaurant and let me know what happened," Bess said.

A short while later, Nancy said good night to Bess, then carried the shopping bags with her new wardrobe up to her room. But as she put the clothes away, her mind wasn't on fashion. Someone was out to get Hal Taylor. Nancy only hoped she could find out who it was before the person did any serious harm.

Bright and early Thursday morning Nancy pulled her blue Mustang into the Channel 9 parking lot.

The news station was housed in an old-fashioned brick building, with graceful white columns ringing the main entrance. Only the battery of antennae and satellite dishes on the roof made it look like a television station.

As she parked next to a Channel 9 news van, Nancy noticed a young man standing beside the van's open sliding door. He appeared to be in his early twenties, and he was struggling under the weight of the camera he was unloading from the van.

Nancy got out of her Mustang, then smoothed the beige woolen skirt she had on beneath her coat. She was also wearing the navy blazer she and Bess had picked out the day before. "Can I give you a hand?" she asked, smiling at the freckle-faced guy. "I'm Nancy Drew, the new intern."

"Marcus Snipes, and thanks a lot," the young man said gratefully. He handed her a stack of videotapes, then balanced the camera on his shoulder. "I'm an intern, too. You have no idea how *heavy* this stuff gets after a while."

Marcus led the way up the steps to the station's lobby, where a receptionist checked Nancy's ID and handed her an identification badge and a parking sticker for her car.

"That'll get you in and out of the station," Marcus explained. "Security's been pretty tight here since all the trouble started."

"Trouble like last night's broadcast?" Nancy asked. Marcus nodded. "What exactly happened?" she prodded.

Marcus lowered his voice as they walked down a long hallway. "Some kind of tape threatening

Hal Taylor was played over the preview monitor —that's a closed-circuit TV that shows what's about to go over the air," he explained.

"What was the crash that we heard?" Nancy asked.

"The producer saw the tape coming over the monitor," Marcus said. "He moved so fast to cut the broadcast that he knocked over a tripod."

At least that hadn't been anything dangerous, Nancy thought. "Do you have any idea what was on the tape?"

Marcus shook his head. "No, but whatever it was had Hal pretty shaken up." He glanced around uneasily as they approached the entrance to the newsroom. "All I know is they're saying it had to be an inside job. Only someone with easy access to the station could have rigged something like that."

As Nancy followed Marcus into the newsroom, she paused for a moment to look around. The large, brightly lit room bustled with activity. Along one wall, an assignment editor was posting story assignments on a chalkboard. Here and there at the desks in the center of the room, reporters were hunched over computers, intently pounding out their stories. Others strode toward a row of tiny booths at the far end of the room.

"Those are the editing booths—that's where they put the news stories together," Marcus explained, following Nancy's gaze. "The reporter lays down the sound track, then the videotape editor adds the pictures and natural sound from the tape we shoot out in the field."

Nancy was impressed by the energy level in the room. "It looks so exciting," she said.

"It *is* exciting," Marcus agreed as he took the pile of tapes back from Nancy. "Ever since I was a little kid I knew I wanted to work in TV. And now I'm doing it!" After showing her where to hang her coat, he pointed across the newsroom to an office that was separated from the newsroom by a glass wall. "That's Otto Liski's office over there—he's the news producer. Good luck on your first day." With a smile, he was off to the other side of the newsroom.

I'll need a lot more than luck, Nancy thought, heading toward the producer's office. She looked through the glass wall and recognized Hal Taylor, who was sprawled in an armchair next to a messy desk. A tall, rangy man in his midthirties was sitting on the edge of the desk. Nancy guessed that he must be Otto Liski. He was questioning a curly haired young woman who stood before him. She seemed to be on the verge of tears.

"We're not accusing you of anything, Valerie," Nancy heard Otto Liski say through the open doorway. "We just want to know how that tape could have been slipped in."

"I swear I don't know," Valerie said, burying her face in her hands. "It just appeared somehow in the pile scheduled for broadcast. I thought it was a last-minute story."

"Mr. Liski?" Nancy interrupted, pausing in the doorway. The producer looked up as she stepped into the office. "I'm Nancy Drew, the new intern," she said, emphasizing the word

14

intern slightly. Only Otto Liski and Hal Taylor were to know of her true mission at the station.

Mr. Liski brightened at the sight of Nancy. "Yes! Good to see you. That'll be all, Valerie," he said to the girl, who looked relieved as she hastened out of the office. The producer closed the door behind her.

"Hal Taylor, this is Nancy Drew. She's the private detective I told you about," Mr. Liski said.

Hal grinned and shook Nancy's hand. She couldn't help noticing his famous dimples.

"You're pretty young and gorgeous to be a private eye, aren't you?" he said.

Nancy felt her pulse quicken involuntarily as she looked into his crystal green eyes. Hal Taylor certainly has looks and charm to spare, she thought.

"Nancy's solved a number of important cases —soon to include this one, I hope," Mr. Liski explained.

"Then I'm glad you're here." Hal's grin faded as he gestured toward a videotape sitting on the desk. "This stuff's really getting out of hand."

"Is that the threatening tape from last night?" Nancy asked.

Hal looked surprised. "I see you already know about that," he said.

"We're trying to keep this incident very quiet, along with the other threats Hal's been receiving," Otto Liski told Nancy. "That's why I was glad when your father recommended calling you. We're trying to avoid contacting the police at this

15

point. Having the public know would only make Hal more of a target."

"I agree," Nancy replied, sitting down on a chair that was next to the desk. "When did the threats start?"

Hal leaned forward and clasped his hands together on the desk. "It's hard to say *exactly* when they started. I mean, periodically I get a few crank calls and letters. When you're a public figure, that kind of stuff comes with the territory," he explained. "But about four weeks ago I started getting letters from someone who seemed to know a lot about me. Where I live, personal habits, that sort of thing. Those are the letters." Hal gestured toward a stack of envelopes next to the tape.

Picking up the letters, Nancy flipped through them. "All typed on the same stationery," she observed. "And there's no postmark. That means they didn't arrive through the mail."

Mr. Liski nodded. "That brings up the most disturbing thing of all. Tell her, Hal."

The anchorman glanced at the letters. "I found them everywhere. On my car windshield, inside my office here at the station—I even found one on the anchor desk," Hal said. "Whoever he is, he could be someone I work next to every day."

Nancy's eyes narrowed thoughtfully. "You say *he*. Is there any reason to suspect it's not a woman?"

Hal Taylor shrugged and shook his head. "I just didn't think of the possibility that it could be a woman. But then, it's hard to think of the idea

16

that *anyone* here could be behind such a thing."

"And you're sure there's a connection between the letters and last night's threat?" Nancy asked.

"The threat on the tape sounded just like the letters," Hal said. He leaned back in his chair and rubbed his eyes wearily. "Here I am, famous investigative reporter—and I can't even figure out who has it in for me."

Nancy glanced at the videotape on the desk. "The first thing I'd like to do is take a look at the tape," she said.

Mr. Liski nodded briskly. "I'll have Valerie play it for you," he said, standing up. "She's the production assistant who was in charge of the tape feed booth last night."

Otto Liski led Nancy through the crowded newsroom. "As our new 'intern,' you'll have free range of the station," he explained quietly to Nancy. "But I warn you—interns are practically slave labor around here, so don't be surprised if you have to do a lot of running, fetching, and carrying."

Liski paused next to one of the desks in the large newsroom, where the curly haired girl he had been talking to when Nancy arrived was sitting. A name plaque on her desk read Valerie Gibson.

"Nancy's going to be Hal's personal assistant," the producer explained to Valerie. "Why don't you show her the tape from last night so that she knows what's been going on here." He handed Valerie the tape that had been on his desk.

17

Valerie nodded glumly. She led Nancy down several hallways until they reached a tiny booth that was jammed with monitors and a control panel.

"I can't believe Otto's making me play this tape again," Valerie moaned. "He and Hal must still blame me for what happened."

"I don't think so," Nancy said gently. She decided to change the subject. "Can you tell me how this feed booth works?"

Valerie explained her job, which was to collect all of the tapes containing the daily news stories. "When we're ready to go on the air, I take each story tape from the stack and put it in here," she said, gesturing toward a bulky tape deck. "This machine sends the story to the control room. From there they press a switch that sends it over the air."

Nancy held up the tape from Otto's office. It was labeled Auto Crash. "And somehow this tape got into the pile?" she asked.

Valerie nodded grimly. "I thought it was a late-breaking story about some accident. Did *I* get a big surprise!" she said, shaking her head with frustration. She flipped a toggle switch on one of the machines. "I just have to rewind what's in here before we play the tape." The machine made a loud, gibberish-type noise as it rewound.

"Did you notice anyone else around this booth last night?" Nancy asked.

Valerie shrugged. "Things get pretty hectic around here right before airtime," she explained.

"Lots of people come and go. I do remember Marilyn Morgan coming into the booth at one point. She was yelling about a glitch—that's a sloppy edit—in one of her stories. Ever since she and Hal broke up, she's always upset about something."

Nancy looked at Valerie in surprise. "Broke up? I thought Hal and Marilyn were a real item."

"*Were* is right," Valerie replied. "They had some kind of big blowup about six weeks ago. Marilyn took it pretty hard, I guess. Anyway, I took her story tape back to the editor, but he couldn't find the glitch she was complaining about."

If there *was* a glitch, Nancy thought. "So you left Marilyn alone in here?" she asked.

"Yeah, she was gone when I got back," Valerie said. "The only other person I remember seeing was one of the engineers, Bill Steghorn. He was working on some wires in the hallway." The whirring sound of the machine stopped. "Now we're ready," she announced.

Valerie switched off the booth's overhead light, then popped the tape into the machine. At once a dark-robed figure appeared on screen, its face hidden by a hideous mask. Then the room was pierced by a strange, menacing voice. The voice growled, "Leave the station, Hal Taylor—*or die!*"

Chapter

Three

THE VOICE and the horrible masked face faded from the screen. Silence filled the booth.

For a moment, Nancy just sat there, stunned. Someone had gone to fiendish lengths to terrify Hal Taylor.

"The voice was obviously electronically disguised," Nancy said at last.

"Yeah, you can't begin to tell who the guy was," Valerie agreed.

Or woman, Nancy thought.

Valerie gave Nancy a puzzled glance. "Why are *you* so interested in this tape, anyway?"

Nancy tried to act casual. "Hal just asked me to look at it for him. I guess because I'm going to be his assistant."

She was relieved when Valerie nodded and busied herself with the control panel. It wouldn't do to blow her cover!

While Valerie's back was turned, Nancy quickly scanned the contents of the booth. She spotted a glint of something shiny between the wall and one of the monitors. Running her hand alongside the monitor, she fished out an odd-looking pen. It was a novelty pen, the kind that companies hand out to promote business. The top of the pen had a liquid capsule containing a miniature truck. When she shook the pen, the truck ran back and forth.

Looking more closely, Nancy saw that most of the lettering on the pen had worn off. She could barely make out the letter *K* on it. She supposed anyone could have dropped it there, but her detective's intuition told her that she had just stumbled across a clue.

Nancy pocketed the pen and thanked Valerie for her help, then returned to the newsroom.

She found Hal Taylor in his office, which was down the hallway from the newsroom. The anchorman's desk was covered with all sorts of unusual knickknacks. He noticed her staring at one of the goofier items, a long-necked bird that endlessly bobbed its head into a glass of water.

"This is Harry the absurd bird," he said, grinning. "Collecting this kind of stuff is a passion of mine. If it's totally useless but fun, it's for me."

Nancy laughed. Then, turning serious, she closed the office door and said, "I wanted to ask you about your relationship with Marilyn Morgan."

Hal took a deep breath and exhaled sharply. "Boy, you don't beat around the bush, do you?" he said. "That's all right, though. I like that. You'd make a good reporter."

"I'll take that as a compliment," Nancy said, and smiled. "Now, about Marilyn . . ."

Hal shifted uncomfortably in his chair. "I guess you've heard Marilyn and I aren't seeing each other anymore." Nancy nodded. "I have to take the blame for the breakup," he continued slowly. "It's just that Marilyn got so competitive with me on major stories. My work is all about competition. I guess I just didn't want my personal life to be that way, too."

Nancy could understand that. It had to be hard working at such a high-pressure job with someone you were dating. "How has she been acting since the breakup?" she asked, sitting down in one of the two chairs next to his desk.

"I guess she took it pretty hard," Hal said. "I've been sort of seeing someone else recently—a waitress who works across town. Marilyn saw us together before we finalized the breakup. That didn't go over too well with her."

"Do you think there could be any connection to the threats against you?" Nancy interrupted.

Hal looked genuinely shocked. "No! Marilyn's been difficult recently, but she'd never risk her career by pulling the kind of stunts we're talking about."

Nancy wasn't convinced, but she decided to let

the matter drop for the moment. "What about a connection to someone outside?" she asked. "Have you been working on any stories that could have provoked a retaliation?"

"As a matter of fact, I am," Hal said. He opened his desk drawer and pulled out a bulky file, which he pushed across the desk to Nancy. "It so happens I've been thinking along those same lines myself."

Hal explained that the attacks had begun while he was developing a story about State Representative Steve Gilbert, a local politician. "Gilbert has a Mr. Clean reputation, but in reality he's been accepting bribes left and right," Hal said. "I found a source who's willing to spill the beans on camera. We go to air with it on Monday. Gilbert's career will be finished, and he knows it—I wouldn't put it past him to be behind something like this."

"So Steve Gilbert knows about the story," Nancy said.

Hal gave her a wry smile. "Let's just say I wouldn't be surprised if he's guessed. My interview with him was rather stormy. Even though I didn't make any direct accusations, I think he understood what I was getting at."

"What about the legal aspects of a story like this?" Nancy asked. "Have you called the police?"

Hal shook his head. "No, this story is what we call enterprise reporting," he explained. "I've collected all the evidence myself. What usually happens in these types of stories is that *after* the story runs, the district attorney will follow up with his own investigation."

Nancy asked for a list of the companies that supposedly had been bribing Steve Gilbert. Hal dug out a sheet of paper that had several names on it. Topping the list was a company called KSM Express.

"KSM is a local trucking company that's been bribing Steve Gilbert to avoid complying with safety and pollution laws," Hal explained. "I'm hitting Gilbert and the company pretty hard in my upcoming report."

"Where can I find Steve Gilbert?" she asked.

"At the statehouse in Springfield," Hal said. He glanced at his watch, then jumped to his feet. "One of our reporters is on his way there to get a few more shots for my story. If we hurry, maybe we can catch him."

The two of them raced out to the parking lot, where a man in his late twenties, with brushed-back sandy hair and dark eyes, was standing beside a camera and some other equipment that was piled next to a news van. The man had a lean, wiry frame and a sour look on his face.

"Gary Krieger, this is my new intern, Nancy Drew," Hal said as he and Nancy stopped next to him. "Since she's training to be a reporter, I want her to get her feet wet on a real assignment."

Gary scowled. "Got anybody else you want me to baby-sit today?" he snapped.

"C'mon, Krieger—" Hal began.

"Thank you, I promise I won't get in the way," Nancy said quickly. Before the reporter could object, she climbed into the backseat. A red-haired young man appeared a moment later and loaded some equipment in beside her.

"Hi, I'm Danny McAnliss," he said to Nancy. He handed her a bulky tape machine that had a cable and microphone attached to it. "I'm the cameraman. Your job will be to monitor the sound levels while we're taping our assignment today—I'll show you how once we get to the state capitol building."

With that, he closed the van's sliding door. Then he and Gary Krieger climbed into the front seats.

The ride started out in an uncomfortable silence. Gary didn't say a word until after he had turned onto the highway leading toward Springfield. Looking at Nancy in the rearview mirror, he said, "I didn't mean to be so rude back there. It's just that Hal Taylor gets on my nerves in a major way."

"Why is that?" Nancy asked.

"I'm doing all his work while he's busy being a pretty boy on camera." Gary slapped the car seat for emphasis. "Like today's assignment. I've done all the legwork on this story about Steve Gilbert. But when it goes on air, you can bet Hal Taylor won't share any of the credit. Isn't that right, Danny?"

Danny, the cameraman, nodded in agreement. "Sharing the limelight isn't Hal Taylor's specialty," he declared. "I say they never should have made him anchor over you, Gary."

"You were supposed to be the anchorman

instead of Hal?" Nancy asked Gary, suddenly alert.

Gary's scowl returned. He didn't reply, but Danny continued talking eagerly. "Gary was up for the job when it came open last year. Then the station's execs went out and brought in Hal Taylor from Seattle. To get better ratings, they said."

"I guess my eyes weren't green enough for the camera," Gary muttered. "What makes it worse is that Hal Taylor isn't worth his salt as a reporter," he added bitterly.

Nancy decided to press Gary for more information about the threats against Hal. "Everyone's talking about what happened on last night's news," she said. "Who do *you* think is threatening him?"

"Someone who's trying to do us all a favor," Gary said, letting out a snort.

Nancy was shocked by the hatred in his voice. It was clear that Hal had made at least one enemy in his rise to the top! As soon as they returned to the station, she intended to look for evidence linking Gary Krieger to the threats against Hal Taylor.

The ride to Springfield took more than two hours. Fortunately, it was a clear day, with no hint of snow. Finally they pulled within sight of the capitol. As the van pulled over the top of the hill, Nancy could see the glittering gold dome of the state capitol building.

Moments later, the van pulled into the sweeping circular drive that led to the statehouse. Gary leapt out of the van even before it came to a complete stop at the curb.

"Can you manage the recorder, Nancy? It's pretty heavy," Danny said as he unloaded some of the equipment.

"No problem," Nancy replied. She grabbed the bulky recorder with its microphone, then followed Gary and Danny up the capitol steps.

Inside the statehouse, Gary led the way down a maze of polished hallways until they reached the large, paneled door of the Senate Transportation Subcommittee Room. They made their way past several politicians and aides who were waiting for the meeting to get started.

Gary turned and looked over his shoulder at Nancy. "Just try not to get in our way while Danny and I are working," he snapped.

"Don't mind him," Danny whispered apologetically as they went into the meeting room. "He always gets this way when he's working on a story."

Nancy helped Danny set up the recorder and check the sound levels. Then she felt someone tap her on the shoulder.

"Nancy Drew, what are *you* doing here?" a familiar voice spoke loudly behind her.

Nancy whirled to find herself staring at Brenda Carlton. The petite, dark-haired reporter was dressed in a white silk blouse, a butternut leather miniskirt, and matching boots. Nancy felt her heart sink.

Brenda was notorious for running sensationalized stories in *Today's Times,* a tabloid that was

27

owned by her father. She was always meddling in Nancy's investigations, and she had come close to wrecking several of them. Now she was gaping at Nancy's microphone with open curiosity.

"Working for WRVH-TV now, are you?" Brenda asked. "Isn't that a bit of a switch for our local girl detec—"

"I could just as easily ask the same of you," Nancy interrupted smoothly. She stifled a sense of panic. Brenda had almost blown her intern cover! "What brings *you* here today?" she asked, hoping to change the focus of the conversation.

Brenda took the bait. "I'm doing an exclusive feature profile on the committee chairman, Steve Gilbert," she said, flicking back her hair with an impeccably manicured nail. "He's a rising star in the political world, you know. Today he's getting an award for legislation he lobbied for on behalf of the trucking industry."

All the votes that money can buy, Nancy thought, recalling Hal's information about the bribes that Steve Gilbert had accepted in exchange for votes that were favorable to the companies paying him. However, she wouldn't blow Hal's scoop by passing along that information to Brenda.

"So are you here working on a case?" Brenda pressed. Nancy was grateful that Gary and Danny were out of earshot, getting a light reading.

"No, I'm just working as an intern until the holidays. I'll tell you all about it later," Nancy promised as she moved away quickly. She pretended to take notes while Steve Gilbert and the other members of the committee entered the room. Brenda looked annoyed, but she didn't follow Nancy across the room.

The committee room resembled a courtroom, with rows of wooden benches for the audience and an elevated dais for the committee members. There weren't many people in the audience—the reporters easily outnumbered the spectators. Gary and Danny had chosen a good spot for their camera setup, directly in front of the chairman's seat.

Nancy noticed a pompous-looking man with a mane of blow-dried silver hair enter the hearing room. When he took the chairman's seat, she knew he was Steve Gilbert. He banged his gavel to bring the meeting to order. He made a few self-serving remarks before accepting an award from a representative from the trucking industry.

When the presentation was finished, Danny clicked off the bright TV camera lights and started disassembling the camera setup. Steve Gilbert glanced in the direction of the Channel 9 news crew.

"I guess I should call a brief recess while our *friends* in the media make their exit," he commented sourly. He banged the gavel again to signal the recess.

Gary just shrugged and continued packing the equipment. Nancy quickly helped Danny fold the cumbersome light stands and pack them away.

This would be a good time to ask him some questions, Nancy decided. She wanted to check out Hal's suspicions that Steve Gilbert was somehow involved in the threats against him. While Gary and Danny had their backs turned, she approached Mr. Gilbert.

"Representative Gilbert?" she began, stopping him as he walked across the room toward the exit.

Gilbert's professional politician's smile faded as he looked at her. "Aren't you with the crew from Channel Nine?" he demanded. "I don't have anything to say to anyone from Hal Taylor's station."

"That's exactly what I want to ask you about," Nancy continued. "Are you aware of what's been happening at the station?"

"I don't know what you're talking about," Steve Gilbert blustered. "And I have no further comment." He brushed past Nancy and headed for the exit.

Nancy felt frustrated as she watched the politician disappear. A straight-on approach wasn't going to work with him, she realized. She'd have to think of another way to gather information.

From across the room, Nancy felt herself caught by Brenda Carlton's calculating stare. The reporter strode across the room toward her.

"Don't tell *me* you're not working on a case, Nancy!" Brenda said. "It's something about Steve Gilbert, isn't it?"

Nancy looked around warily. She could see Gary Krieger staring curiously in their direction. She decided to turn the tables on Brenda.

"What's the matter, Brenda," she said, "can't you find your *own* stories to write about? Or is it that you can't stand the thought of my competing with you as a TV reporter?"

Brenda's mouth fell open. "Do you think I'm jealous just because you're working in TV and I'm not?" she asked, a defensive glint in her dark eyes. "No way! People are always telling me I'd be a natural on TV!" With that, she turned on her heel and stomped off.

Nancy breathed a sigh of relief. She'd thrown Brenda off the trail—for the moment.

When she rejoined Gary and Danny by the camera equipment, Nancy found the two men hunched over, listening intently to a mobile phone that the reporter was holding up to his ear.

"What's going on?" Nancy asked. From the tense look on their faces, she was afraid there had been another attack on Hal Taylor.

"It's the station," Gary announced. "We've got an emergency!"

Chapter

Four

WHAT'S THE EMERGENCY?" Nancy asked, quickly moving to help carry the equipment back outside. "Does it have anything to do with Hal Taylor?"

"Shh!" Gary warned as they passed another camera crew, which was taping an interview in the hallway. As soon as they were safely past the other reporters, Gary sprinted ahead.

"An apartment building caught fire over on Market Street in Springfield," he explained to Nancy in a low voice. "If we hurry, we'll be the first ones on the scene."

Nancy helped Danny heave the equipment into the back of the van, then turned around and looked for Gary. Strangely, the reporter was suddenly nowhere to be found.

"Where'd Gary go?" she asked Danny.

The cameraman merely shrugged and smiled mysteriously. "Taking care of business" was all he said.

Frowning, Nancy walked down the row of news vans that were parked alongside the curb. Then she spotted Gary—he was hunched over the rear wheel of one of the vehicles. He was using a metal instrument to let the air out of the tire!

"Why are you doing that?" Nancy asked angrily. She couldn't believe that he was actually trying to sabotage the other station's news van.

Gary Krieger looked up at Nancy. "This is an old reporter's trick," he explained. "It slows down the competition." Once the tire was deflated, he jumped to his feet and dashed back to the Channel 9 van. Nancy couldn't believe his unethical action! She had no choice but to follow him back to the van. But when they got back to the station, she felt that she would have to tell Otto Liski about the incident.

Gary drove at breakneck speed back to Market Street. When they arrived at the fire scene, puffs of ashy smoke could be seen rising from the apartment building, but no flames were visible. Nancy and Danny waited in the van, while Gary dashed off to talk with a couple of fire officials who were standing around. The reporter returned, disappointment clearly written on his face.

"It's only a puffer," he announced. "Lots of smoke but no major injuries or property damage."

"But that's *good,* right?" Nancy protested.

Gary Krieger shrugged. "Not for me. I thought I had the lead story for tonight's newscast. This story won't even make it into the lineup. It was a total waste of time."

Nancy shook her head as she climbed back into the news van. She thought about Gary's behavior and his jealousy of Hal Taylor. It was clear that he was a man who knew few limits when it came to pursuing a news assignment. The question was—did Gary Krieger know any limits when it came to pursuing the job of anchorman?

"I heard someone say that the incident on the news last night must have been an inside job," Nancy commented once they'd pulled away from the fire. "It's sort of scary to think of someone like that working at the station."

She watched Gary carefully, but he simply shrugged. "Liski and Hal blew that whole thing way out of proportion," he said. "I think it was just a stupid prank—no big deal."

"Like that clever prank you pulled on that rival news van?" Nancy asked in an even tone.

Gary shot her a look, but Danny laughed out loud. "She's got you there, Gary," he said teasingly. "Krieger's always in hot water with management because of his practical jokes," he continued, turning to look at Nancy. "Gary, remember that time you switched our blooper

tape with Hal's lead story on the newscast? Whoo
boy, was Liski mad about *that* one!"

"Shut up, Danny," Gary snapped. Nancy sat
back triumphantly. So Gary had a prankster
history that included switching tapes! He was
now looming larger as a suspect in Nancy's mind.

Nancy sought out Otto Liski in his office as
soon as she arrived back at the TV station. To her
surprise, the producer seemed to dismiss Gary's
sabotage of the rival news van.

"Krieger's the journalistic equivalent of a
trained attack dog," Mr. Liski said. "Every de-
cent news operation has a reporter like him—
someone who'll do almost anything to get the
story and get it first. It's such a competitive
business that we have to rely on his kind, like it or
not."

"What about the fact that he wanted Hal's job
as anchorman?" Nancy asked. "That would give
him a strong motive in the threats—and he has a
history of switching tapes on the air." She quickly recounted the story of the blooper tape incident.

Otto Liski shook his head. "That was just an
April fool joke that Krieger pulled," the producer
said. "Anyway, he wouldn't gain anything by
Hal's leaving. Even though *he* seems to think so,
he was never a serious contender last year for the
job. He doesn't have the right qualities to become
an anchor. A good anchorman has to project a
smooth, friendly image—the total opposite of
Krieger's style."

Nancy had a feeling Gary didn't know that, however. Before she could say anything more, a knock sounded on the door, and Valerie stepped into the office.

"Marilyn's been acting up again," she told Otto Liski, a worried expression on her face. "The hairdresser called in sick today, and Marilyn's saying she won't go on the air without a hot comb."

Mr. Liski sighed and shook his head. "Marilyn's a real prima donna," he explained to Nancy. "But the viewers love her, so we try to keep her happy." He turned back to Valerie. "You'll have to beg, borrow, or steal a hot comb from someone. Try Murphy over in sports. He's always fussing with that lion's mane of his."

"I'd be happy to track down a comb for her," Nancy quickly offered. She was eager for a chance to find out what, if anything, Marilyn knew about the attacks on Hal.

On her way to find Murphy, Nancy did a quick survey of Krieger's desk. Since it was in the middle of the open, crowded newsroom, there was not much chance for sleuthing. The other reporters' desks were covered with photos and assorted memorabilia, she noted, but Krieger's was bare except for his computer terminal and a collection of journalism awards. He didn't seem to have many interests outside the news business.

Nancy found Mike Murphy in the sports department. True to Mr. Liski's word, the sportscaster was applying a final spritz of hairspray on his wavy blond hair. He was happy to lend Nancy his hot comb.

"Just be careful when you give it to Marilyn," he warned jokingly. "You might find some claw marks when you pull back your hand."

"Is she that bad?"

Murphy shrugged. "Recently she has been," he said. "It's just a case of that old saying—no fury like a woman scorned. She took it pretty hard when Hal broke off their engagement."

"I didn't realize they were actually engaged," Nancy said in surprise. She wondered why Hal hadn't mentioned his engagement to Marilyn. No wonder she'd gotten so upset when he broke up with her!

"They were going to announce their engagement in the newspaper," Murphy said, in response to Nancy's question. "Then Hal got cold feet or came to his senses, depending on how you look at it. Marilyn's been busy making everyone miserable ever since."

Murphy put the hairspray back into his desk drawer. "Anyway, I heard that she might jump ship pretty soon, so she'll be someone else's problem."

"You mean leave the station?" Nancy asked. This was definitely a day for surprises.

"Yep," Murphy said. "I heard she was negotiating with one of the biggies—the national networks," he explained. "She brings in great ratings, although why the viewers like her *I'll* never understand."

"Marilyn doesn't seem like a very serious newsperson," Nancy agreed.

"*None* of us look very serious these days with our new happy talk format," Murphy said. "Marilyn's just better at the chitchat than most of us."

After thanking Murphy for the hot comb, Nancy set off to find Marilyn's office. She found it tucked away at the end of the same hallway where Hal's office was located.

Nancy paused just outside the door, which was half-open. She could hear the anchorwoman talking in hushed tones. Nancy was about to knock on the door when she heard Marilyn's voice rise in anger.

"I don't care," Marilyn said. "I'll murder Hal before I let him humiliate me with that girl!"

Chapter

Five

A MOMENT LATER, Nancy heard Marilyn bang down the phone.

Nancy stood frozen, unsure of what to do. Finally she cleared her throat and tapped on the door, then stepped into the doorway. Marilyn looked up at her with a flustered expression.

"What do you want?" she snapped. Then she saw the hot comb in Nancy's hand. "Oh, put it down over there," she said, gesturing toward a small vanity table in the corner. "And go get me a ham sandwich and some coffee while you're at it—black with two sugars."

"No problem," Nancy said, and left Marilyn's office. Any questions would have to wait. She took several wrong turns but eventually reached the commissary. Seeing the sandwiches and salads at the snack bar made Nancy's stomach growl. She suddenly realized that she hadn't eaten lunch. She wolfed down half a tuna sandwich, then headed back to Marilyn's office with the ham sandwich and coffee.

Marilyn's office was empty when Nancy got there. Nancy glanced up and down the hallway to make sure no one was coming, then conducted a quick survey of the office. First her gaze came to rest on a three-drawer file cabinet next to Marilyn's desk. She tried one of the drawers, but it was locked. Reaching into her jacket pocket, she withdrew a tiny leather case that contained her lock-picking tools. The file drawer gave easily after she fiddled with the lock for a few moments.

Inside the top drawer, Nancy found a stack of manila file folders. She flipped through the folders, looking for anything that might link Marilyn to the threatening tape or letters that Hal had received. One of the folders was marked Personal. Opening it, Nancy discovered a stack of letters and notes. They were all written to Marilyn from Hal. The first few notes were warm and loving—obviously love letters. But as Nancy continued reading, the tone of the letters changed. They sounded terse, even angry. Hal accused Marilyn of acting vindictive following their breakup.

Continuing to look through the file, Nancy found a series of letters to Marilyn from a major network. Murphy was right—Marilyn was negotiating for a new job with a big increase in salary.

That made her more of a suspect in Nancy's eyes. If Marilyn was about to leave the station, she wouldn't care about any negative effects sabotage might have on her show's ratings.

Nancy tensed as she heard a noise coming from the hallway. She quickly replaced the letters in the file and locked the drawer. By the time Marilyn strode in a moment later, Nancy was pretending to stir the coffee she had brought for the anchorwoman.

"Why are you still here?" Marilyn demanded, taking the cup from Nancy.

"I was wondering if you needed anything else," Nancy replied.

Nancy's response seemed to mollify the anchorwoman. She took a sip of coffee, then asked in a softer tone, "What are you, a new intern?"

"Yes, my name is Nancy Drew. I've been assigned to work for Hal Taylor," she said, then waited for a reaction from Marilyn.

She didn't have long to wait. Marilyn's expression turned calculating, and her eyes swept over Nancy in a frankly appraising look. "You should do well. He evidently likes them young and pretty." She turned away from Nancy with a dismissive gesture.

Just then there was a tap on Marilyn's door, and a tall, bearded man in his fifties appeared in the doorway. He wore blue overalls and had an assortment of small tools hanging from his belt. He was holding out an elegant crystal table lamp to Marilyn.

"I finished rewiring your lamp," he said in a soft voice that contrasted with his husky appearance.

Marilyn clasped her hands together. "Oh, thank you, Bill," she said, looking pleased. She took the lamp and set it on her desk. Then she seemed to realize that Nancy was still standing there. "Oh—Bill, this is Nancy Drew," she said, almost as an afterthought.

"I'm a new intern," Nancy said, shaking his hand.

"Bill Steghorn, chief engineer," he told her.

"Bill's been an angel, helping me out with little chores around my house," Marilyn said. "I don't know what I would have done without him, ever since Hal and I broke up."

Bill patted her shoulder. "It'll be okay," he said gently.

Nancy left Marilyn's office, puzzling over Marilyn Morgan's mercurial nature. She could be cold and demanding one instant, and soft and vulnerable the next. One thing was for sure—Nancy would definitely press Hal for more information about the vindictiveness he referred to in his letters to Marilyn.

She found Hal in the news studio, sitting at the studio anchor desk, reading over some last-minute copy. When she told him that she wanted to talk about Marilyn, he covered up his microphone with his hand.

"You never know when you might have an open mike—anyone could be listening," he explained in a low voice.

Hal refused to give any details about Marilyn's behavior, though. "It goes against my gentleman's code of honor," he explained. "Suffice it to say that she was very difficult at one point, but all that blew over a while back."

A harried-looking floor director rushed over to Nancy and thrust a pile of papers at her. "Are you the new intern?" he asked. "Good," he continued without waiting for her reply. "These are the scripts for the show. I want you to tape them together end-to-end so that we can run them through the TelePrompTer." He gestured toward a machine directly in front of the anchor desk.

Nancy found a roll of tape and quickly pieced the script together. When she returned the script to the floor director, she asked, "Are they taking extra precautions for the news shows tonight?"

"Yes," the director said. "We don't want a replay of last night's incident." He raked a hand through his wiry hair. "I hate having a guard around, though. It puts everyone on edge—especially me."

While he placed the script next to the Tele-PrompTer, Nancy walked over to the security guard. "Mr. Liski asked me to find out whether you'd seen anything suspicious so far," she said to him. Although the producer *hadn't* asked her to check, Nancy felt she would have a better chance of getting information if she used Mr. Liski's name. The guard didn't seem to hear her. "Hey!" she said more sharply, tapping him on the arm.

The guard looked startled. Then he removed a pair of tiny headphones from his ears. "What? Sorry, I was just listening to the radio," he apologized. "It gets kind of boring, standing here for hours on end."

Nancy groaned inwardly. It was clear that this guard would be pretty useless in a real emergency!

"Have you seen anything suspicious?" she asked again. The guard shook his head and replaced his earphones.

Sighing, Nancy gave up. Turning her attention back to Marilyn Morgan, she decided to see what Otto Liski knew about her bitterness toward Hal.

She found the producer in the control room, talking to Bill Steghorn. "Bill, you've got to have your people fix the lighting over Hal Taylor," Otto Liski was saying. "It's been really unflattering recently. He's looking a little green around the gills."

"I don't think it's the lighting," Bill replied. "But I'll speak to Clay Jurgenson about it—he's in charge of the lighting this afternoon." He spotted Nancy and gave her a friendly nod on his way out of the control room. "Too bad Hal isn't easy to light, like Marilyn," he mumbled.

When Nancy told Mr. Liski that she needed to speak with him privately, they retreated to a prop room just off one of the hallways leading from the newsroom. It was filled with puppets and sets from an afternoon children's show.

"Let me just move this," Mr. Liski said, sweeping aside an oversize panda bear from a stool. He sat down, then looked questioningly at Nancy. "Now, what did you want to ask me?"

Nancy perched on an oversize rocking chair. Without divulging the details of her lock-picking, she described what she had discovered about Marilyn's vindictive behavior toward Hal. Otto Liski listened carefully, then shook his head.

"I just can't believe that Marilyn could be behind these threats," he said firmly. "She's difficult, but she's not *that* kind of difficult. No, I have other worries where Marilyn is concerned," he continued. "I've been hearing rumors that she's negotiating with a national network. That could spell disaster for our ratings."

"Those rumors are true—I've seen the letters from the network," Nancy told him. "If you ask me, that gives her even more motivation to destroy Hal and this newscast."

"That's a good point," Mr. Liski admitted. He rubbed his chin distractedly. "We'll have to talk about this later, though. Right now I have to check the story lineup for the news."

Nancy followed the producer back to the news studio, then remembered her promise to call Bess with an update. She saw an empty office with a phone in it. Bess's shift at the restaurant didn't start for another hour, so Nancy called her at home.

"Thank goodness nothing else terrible has happened," Bess said after Nancy had filled her in on the day's events. "Oh—I forgot to tell you yesterday, but I think one of the girls I work with knows Hal."

45

It might not be much of a lead, thought Nancy, but it couldn't hurt to follow up on it. "See if she knows anything about the attacks, okay?" she asked.

"Sure," Bess told her. "By the way, isn't Ned coming home soon?"

"Tomorrow," Nancy said, and smiled. She hoped she'd be able to see him over the weekend —case or no case. After promising to talk to Bess again soon, she hung up.

As she was walking past the news taping studio, the floor director called to her, "Over here, Nancy!"

As she went over to him, she noticed that the atmosphere had become thick with tension. Even the guard had taken off his headphones and was watching alertly.

"I need your help," the floor director told her. "Hal and Marilyn have controls by their feet that automatically run the script through the Tele-PrompTer, like computer paper. But sometimes the paper jams, so you have to yank it a bit. I need you to stand by the TelePrompTer."

"Sure," Nancy said, and went over to stand by the machine.

Marilyn walked onto the set and took her seat next to Hal at the anchor desk. She was dressed in a royal blue knit suit, with her hair sleeked back into a sophisticated French twist.

Picking up a stack of papers in front of her, she glanced through the script. She made a face and clicked on her in-studio microphone.

"Otto, this is the third time in a row this week that Hal has introduced the lead story," she complained. The sound system amplified her words so that they boomed loudly across the studio.

From his position inside the glass-enclosed control room opposite her, Otto Liski threw up his hands in a helpless gesture. "We gave Hal all the lead-ins on the crime series because he's been working on the story with the reporter," his reply came echoing back.

"I don't care *who* the reporter is. I want my share of lead-ins," Marilyn said firmly. "It's in my contract, remember?"

"I remember." Mr. Liski sighed. "Hal, switch your copy with Marilyn, okay?"

Hal Taylor muttered under his breath, but he tore the top page off his script and handed it to Marilyn. She accepted the paper with a tight smile.

"Fifteen seconds to air," the floor director announced. "Live shots on standby."

When the director signaled to Marilyn, the anchorwoman's expression dissolved into a broad smile. "Good afternoon, this is the Channel Nine Four O'Clock News. I'm Marilyn Morgan," she said.

"And I'm Hal Taylor," Hal announced with an equally engaging grin. Their faces bore no trace of the unpleasantness of a moment earlier.

Marilyn read the introduction to the top story, an investigative piece on the housing industry by reporter Gary Krieger. As the news broadcast progressed without incident, the nervous tension on the set gradually began to dissipate.

Nancy had her hands full running the temperamental TelePrompTer, but she was also closely watching Marilyn's and Hal's performances. When the camera lights were on, the anchor couple acted perfectly cordial toward each other, chatting amiably between the various news segments that they were introducing. Off camera, however, they lapsed into stony silence.

When the last story, which Nancy had learned was always called the kicker, concluded, Hal and Marilyn signed off by saying goodbye to the viewers. Then the program was off the air.

The production crew burst into spontaneous applause—everyone, including Nancy, was relieved that the broadcast had ended without incident.

"See if you can try not to step on my lead-ins again on the six o'clock news, Hal," Marilyn commented acidly. Without another word, she stalked off the set.

Hal stared after her before leaving the set. As he headed toward the hallway leading to his office, Nancy joined him.

"Let's go over that assignment you were telling me about," Nancy said. In case anyone else was listening, she wanted to make sure she sounded like an intern. Hal didn't even seem to notice her comment.

"I might have to start a new career as a bus driver," he grumbled as they rounded a corner.

"Between Marilyn's cold shoulder and these threats I've been receiving, this job is beginning to get to me."

Nancy sniffed as she suddenly picked up an acrid smell. She looked up ahead—then stopped short.

"Look out, Hal!" she exclaimed, grabbing his arm. She pointed down the hallway, and Hal stopped and stared.

Thick black smoke was seeping out from underneath his office door!

Chapter

Six

"STAY BACK, HAL—there could be an explosion!" Nancy exclaimed.

Motioning for Hal to stay behind her, she grabbed a fire extinguisher that was hanging on the wall. Both of them were already beginning to cough from the smoke. Hurrying to the door, Nancy ran her hand over it to check for intense heat. It didn't seem too hot, so she threw open the door.

Flames were licking across Hal's desk, but the fire hadn't yet spread very far. Nancy pulled the pin on the fire extinguisher, releasing a whooshing spray of foam that quickly snuffed out the fire.

Seconds later Hal was in the office with her, sadly regarding the smoking remains of his desk. He tapped his favorite glass bird, which was now dripping with ash and foam. The bird obligingly bobbed its head into the now-empty cup of water.

"Well, at least Harry made it," Hal said, but his voice cracked with tension.

The smell of lighter fluid hung in the air. There was no question that this fire had been deliberately set, Nancy realized. Belatedly, a smoke alarm in the hallway began ringing. Several other people rushed into Hal's office, some carrying fire extinguishers.

Nancy glanced up at the ceiling. "The smoke alarm in here has been ripped out," she said. Turning to Hal, she asked, "What did you lose from your desk?"

Hal gingerly sifted through the blackened, smoking material on his desk, then opened all the drawers. He shook his head. "All my notes on the bribery case—I can re-create those, but the tape I was working on was stolen out of my locked drawer. They must have jimmied it."

In a whisper only Nancy could hear, he added, "Fortunately, I have the master tape locked up at my house. I had a sneaking suspicion that something like this might happen."

"Whoever set this fire wanted to send you a message," Nancy said grimly. "Otherwise, they would have just stolen the stuff."

Just then the security guard burst into the

room and took a look at the damage. He reacted by making a low whistle.

"Did you see anything?" Hal asked the guard.

The guard shook his head. "No, but I was keeping an eye on the set, not back here," he reported.

"*I* saw something." A tall, blond man who had been standing in the doorway stepped forward. He was wearing a technician's uniform. "I'm Clay Jurgenson," he said. "I saw someone running away from Hal's office. The person was wearing a Channel Nine jacket."

"Was it a man or a woman?" Nancy asked.

Clay Jurgenson shook his head. "Sorry. I couldn't tell. I just saw the logo on the back of the jacket as the person disappeared around the corner. I didn't think anything of it until I heard the smoke alarm ringing."

The sound of a sarcastic chuckle made Nancy glance toward the doorway. Gary Krieger was leaning insolently against the doorjamb. He, too, was wearing a Channel 9 jacket.

"Someone wearing a station jacket—that must narrow down the list of suspects to about twenty or thirty people," Gary said mockingly. He eyed Hal's charred desk. "I guess we have ourselves another puffer," he sneered. "Lots of smoke, not much damage." He took off down the hallway without another word.

Nancy couldn't believe that Gary could be so callous toward Hal. She recalled Gary's behavior during the apartment fire earlier that afternoon. Was it possible that he was behind *this* blaze?

"I hate to admit it, but Krieger's right—we *all* own station jackets," Hal said.

He looked up as Otto Liski appeared in his office. "Okay, that's enough gawking. Back to work, everyone." Once the area had cleared out, he shut Hal's door and stared glumly at the ruined desk.

"This is getting worse," he said. "Before now we've only been getting threats against Hal. Now there's been an actual attack."

"I think it's time to let the police in on what's been going on," Nancy advised him. "I've worked with Chief McGinnis on other cases. He and his men can work very discreetly when necessary, so maybe word of the attack won't leak to the press."

Otto Liski looked from Nancy to Hal, then shook his head. "I don't want to risk having the public get wind of this," he said. "What can we do, short of calling the police?"

Nancy thought for a moment. "So far we know that the arsonist is someone on the inside— there's too much security for an outsider to be pulling this off, plus Clay saw someone wearing the station jacket."

She was thinking out loud, piecing her thoughts together as she went. "And since Hal's notes on the Steve Gilbert story were destroyed, it seems likely that the person is trying to prevent Hal from running his story. I need to check out whether there's any connection between Gilbert and anyone at the station." Looking at Mr. Liski, she said, "I'll need to review your personnel records as soon as possible."

The producer rubbed his chin thoughtfully. "Those files are supposed to be confidential," he said slowly. "But under the circumstances I'll make an exception."

Soon Nancy was sitting in an empty cubicle, poring over the résumés and other personal documents of the Channel 9 staff. She paid close attention to the files belonging to Marilyn Morgan and Gary Krieger.

Marilyn's file revealed little. She had worked at stations all over the Midwest before coming to WRVH and had risen rapidly from weather reporter to anchorwoman. Gary Krieger's résumé contained an interesting footnote. Under the Hobbies and Interests section, he had described himself as a volunteer fire fighter. It wasn't enough to link him to the blaze in Hal's office, but it told Nancy that he was someone who knew his way around fire.

It took Nancy over two hours to go through all the files, so she had missed the six o'clock news. When she returned the files to Mr. Liski's office, he told her that there had been no incidents during the broadcast. "Did you find anything?" he asked.

"Nothing conclusive," she told him. "I'd like to question Bill Steghorn, though. Valerie said that he was working outside the tape feed booth last night. Maybe he saw something. In any case, he's also a possible suspect."

"You'll probably find him somewhere back in

the equipment area," Liski said. He pointed to an open utility door. "It's down that hallway. Keep turning right until you reach a big computer room."

Nancy wandered down the cool, dim passageways of the station's equipment area to look for the engineer. In the semidarkness, she was suddenly uncomfortably aware of the feeling that someone was watching her.

"Lost your way?"

Nancy jumped as Bill Steghorn emerged from the shadows. In the gloom, his bearded face with his heavy eyebrows looked vaguely threatening. Then he smiled, and the menacing look was gone.

"No, I came back here to find you," Nancy replied. "Hal Taylor asked me to pick up some equipment for him."

At the mention of Hal's name, Bill Steghorn's expression darkened slightly. "Hal Taylor," he said with distaste. "If you're here for long, you'll find out that he isn't exactly a favorite with the production people."

Nancy pretended to be sympathetic. "I gather he's not a favorite with a *lot* of people around here," she said.

Bill shrugged, then reached down to grab his tool kit and an equipment bag from the floor. Now that Nancy's eyes had adjusted to the dimness, she saw some fresh duct tape around a cable he had apparently been working on.

"You can never fool the production people about who the good and bad on-air people are,"

Bill told Nancy. "We know because we're the ones who make them look good." They walked together down the hallway until they stood in front of a row of lockers.

"Hal's a lightweight," the engineer went on dismissively. "Now, Marilyn Morgan, on the other hand—she's a good reporter and a great lady." He set down his bags and opened his locker.

Remembering that Bill Steghorn was a possible suspect, Nancy quickly scanned his locker for anything that might link him to the recent attacks against Hal. She didn't see a typewriter or any kerosene, but she noticed that the inside of his locker door was covered with publicity photos of Marilyn.

Bill felt her curious gaze. His heavy eyebrows drew together in a frown as he placed some tools on his locker shelf. Then he slammed the door shut. "What was it that you needed to pick up for Hal?" he asked Nancy.

"Just another clip mike," Nancy improvised. "His other one was destroyed in the fire in his office, and he used someone else's for the six o'clock news."

"Yeah, someone seems to really have it in for him," Bill said, handing her a microphone from his equipment bag.

"No one seems to have seen anything suspicious, though," Nancy commented, hoping to draw the engineer into revealing whether he'd seen anything the previous evening.

"Yeah, I was working outside the tape booth last night, and I didn't see a soul except for Marilyn and that production assistant, Valerie," he commented. "Beats me how they got that screwball tape into the broadcast."

Nancy thanked the engineer for the microphone, then returned to the newsroom. It was nearly seven-thirty, and she suddenly realized that she was famished again. She didn't know how much more she could find out about the sabotage, so she decided to call it a day and head home for some dinner.

On her way out, Nancy passed by Hal's office. The anchorman wasn't there, but a couple of fire fighters were sifting through the ashes, looking for evidence of arson.

As she passed through the lobby, Nancy felt an arm link smoothly through hers. She found herself staring into the sparkling green eyes of Hal Taylor.

"I always take my new assistants out for a bite to eat on their first day." He grinned. "Since you're such a special intern, why don't we make it a special meal? Let's say, someplace like Le St. Tropez?" Le St. Tropez was one of River Heights's more romantic and elegant restaurants. Its dining room had a stone fireplace and an intimate atmosphere.

The color rose in Nancy's cheeks as she felt the warmth of Hal's touch. "Isn't that a pretty cozy spot for a business meeting?" she teased.

"It's not business I have in mind at the moment," Hal teased right back. "Besides, they have the world's best beef Wellington. Trust me."

Nancy felt herself being propelled forward by the force of Hal's charm. Before she knew it, the two of them were in Nancy's Mustang on their way to the restaurant. Hal whistled appreciatively as she maneuvered through traffic.

"A bright, beautiful girl who drives her sports car like a pro," he said, smiling. "Is there anything you *don't* do well?"

"Give me a minute and I'll think of something," Nancy returned. It's no wonder that Hal Taylor is so popular, she thought—he's irresistible!

The maître d' greeted Hal warmly—the news anchor was obviously a regular. He showed them to a private booth at the back of the restaurant. After they were seated, Nancy tried to discuss the case, but Hal wanted no part of it.

"I'd much rather talk about you," he said. "How did you become a private investigator?"

He listened while she described some of the more famous cases she'd worked on. Then he said, "I meant it earlier today when I said you'd make a great reporter. Have you ever thought of a career on the air?"

"Being a reporter seems pretty glamorous, but I guess I'm really a detective at heart," she told Hal.

"Speaking of hearts," Hal said softly. "Is there a handsome boyfriend lurking in the wings?"

"Yes," Nancy answered truthfully. She felt a guilty stab of conscience as she thought about Ned. After all, he would be coming home to see her the next night. What would he think if he could see her having a romantic dinner with Hal Taylor?

Hal leaned back and smiled ruefully. "I suppose it was too much to hope that you'd be fabulous *and* unattached," he said. "I'm not really free, either, I guess. I'm still seeing the waitress I told you about. And I still haven't been able to sort out my feelings about Marilyn. Sometimes I think we news types aren't meant to be in a stable relationship," he finished.

"Why do you say that?" Nancy asked.

"It's tough being involved with a reporter," Hal explained. "I guess we journalists are really married to our careers more than to anything else. That was one thing Marilyn understood. I kind of miss that about her," he added wistfully.

After dinner Nancy dropped Hal off at the station. She shook her head as she watched him disappear into the building. He didn't seem to know what he was looking for in a relationship. And that meant that Hal had the potential to be dangerous to a woman's heart!

When Nancy arrived home, she spotted a note on the refrigerator. "Gone to see my sister. Back soon. Love, Hannah."

Nancy dropped her purse on the kitchen table and made herself a cup of cocoa. She was just settling down to drink it when the phone rang. It was Bess. Her friend's tone sounded urgent.

"Hurry over to the Schooner Deck as soon as you can," Bess said in an excited voice. "I've found out something important about your case!"

Chapter

Seven

What is it, Bess?" Nancy asked, feeling a burst of adrenaline race through her.

"I can't talk right now—the manager is breathing down my neck," Bess replied nervously. "Just hurry over. He'll be off duty in a few minutes, and then we can talk."

Nancy didn't waste a second. Twenty minutes later, she pulled up to the River Heights café where Bess worked. By now it was after ten, and the restaurant was practically deserted.

"Nancy!" Bess cried as soon as Nancy came through the door. She grabbed Nancy's hand and led her to a corner table where a dark-haired girl was sitting. The girl was also wearing a waitress's uniform.

"This is Rita Greenburg," Bess said, introducing Nancy. "Rita works here in the afternoons. She's the girl I mentioned to you—the one who knows Hal Taylor."

"Pleased to meet you, Rita." Nancy shook the girl's hand. "Now, tell me what's going on," she said to Bess.

"I found out this afternoon that she not only *knows* Hal—she's been dating him for the past couple of months," Bess said.

"And I can tell you an *earful* about that witch Marilyn Morgan," Rita added glumly. "She's been making my life totally miserable."

Nancy sat down. "You'd better start from the beginning," she advised.

Rita nodded and nervously twisted a paper napkin in her fingers. She described how she and Hal had met when he came in the restaurant to order lunch. "He seemed so glamorous. I liked him right away," she explained. "We'd only gone out a couple of times when I got this nasty phone call from Marilyn. You should have heard the names she called me!"

"What did you do?" Nancy asked.

"I just hung up on her," Rita replied. "But then one day she showed up here at the restaurant and tried to get me fired! She told the manager I was unprofessional. Thank goodness he didn't believe her."

"When did that happen?" Nancy wanted to know.

Rita thought for a moment. "Over a month ago," she replied. "After she couldn't get me fired, she seemed to back off. But recently I've been getting these hang-up calls late at night. Somehow I just know it's Marilyn calling again."

"Sounds like she's really the vindictive type," Nancy commented.

"I'll say," Bess chimed in. "Talk about not knowing when to take the hint that the relationship is over!"

Rita went on to explain that she was considering breaking off her relationship with Hal. "It's partly the Marilyn thing, partly the fact that he's always so busy," she explained. "I guess it's just not meant to be."

Considering how confused Hal seemed to be about romance, Rita's decision seemed like a good one, Nancy thought. "Thanks for telling me about your experience with Marilyn," she told Rita. "I know it must be hard to talk about."

Rita sighed and nodded. "This whole thing with Hal and Marilyn has got me really shaken," she said. "It makes me wonder how far she'll go for revenge."

Nancy had been wondering the same thing. "Did you ever receive any threatening notes from Marilyn?" she asked. If so, she could compare them to the threats Hal had been receiving.

"No. Just nasty messages on the answering machine," Rita replied. "That was bad enough."

After thanking Rita for her help, Nancy said goodbye and walked to the front door of the restaurant with Bess. "Can you go with me to the statehouse tomorrow on a little mission?" she asked.

"I don't have to be here until five o'clock tomorrow, so I'm free," Bess replied. "What do you have in mind?"

"Whoever is behind these attacks may have a connection to that politician Steve Gilbert," Nancy explained. "I want to go to his office tomorrow to see what we can dig up."

"Count me in," Bess said with a smile.

"Thanks," Nancy said, giving her friend a hug goodbye.

As she drove home, Nancy mentally reviewed the case. So far, she had three strong suspects—Marilyn Morgan, Gary Krieger, and Steve Gilbert. The fire in Hal's office pointed to Steve Gilbert, since the tape that had been stolen would have exposed him. But Nancy knew that someone on the inside would have to be cooperating with the politician to pull off such an attack.

Could Marilyn Morgan or Gary Krieger be in league with Gilbert? Hopefully, she and Bess would find out the answer to that question the next day.

Friday morning was cold and blustery, but Nancy was grateful there was no snow as she and Bess made the long drive to the statehouse in Springfield. Nancy brought a notebook and a tape recorder with her.

"My official excuse for coming here today is to do some research at the senate library for one of Hal's stories," Nancy explained to Bess after they found a place to park near the impressive building. "But we'll have plenty of time to check out Gilbert's office."

"What do you hope to find there?" Bess asked as they made their way toward the sweeping marble stairs of the statehouse.

"With any luck, we'll find out some information that will link Gilbert to one of the suspects at Channel Nine," Nancy said.

Inside the statehouse, Nancy and Bess found a young senate page who directed them to Steve Gilbert's legislative office. It was just before noon, and the hallway was beginning to fill with legislators and office workers headed for lunch.

Nancy spotted the representative leaving with an assistant. She quickly bent her head over a drinking fountain so that Gilbert wouldn't recognize her.

"Let's go to Hornby's for lunch," she heard him say as he passed. "I could go for their pastrami on rye."

Good, Nancy thought. Steve Gilbert would probably be gone for at least an hour. "Okay, Bess," she said when he had disappeared around the corner. "I need to get into Gilbert's office while he's gone. Time to do your thing!"

"All right," Bess said, grinning. She tossed back her golden hair with a flourish and marched into Steve Gilbert's outer office, where a young legislative aide sat at a desk.

"Can I help you?" the handsome young man asked with a smile.

"Oh, I *hope* so." Bess beamed at the aide. "I was on a tour with my high school class, and I seem to have gotten lost. I've been wandering around for hours. Could you help me find the senate chambers?"

"I'd love to take you there myself, but I'm really not supposed to leave the office unattended," the aide replied apologetically.

Bess leaned slightly toward him over the desk. "I'm just so *fascinated* by politics," she said, looking deep into the man's eyes.

"I—I guess it wouldn't hurt to leave the office for a second," the aide said. He flashed Bess a bright smile as he stood up. Bess winked at Nancy as she walked past her with Steve Gilbert's assistant in tow.

Now Nancy had her chance! She slipped into the representative's waiting room, then hurried over to a door marked Private. It was locked, but Nancy quickly got it open with her special tools.

Steve Gilbert's office was furnished with a heavy oak desk, a leather couch and matching chairs, file cabinets, and bookshelves. Nancy quickly went to work, searching for anything that might tie the man to the threats against Hal Taylor.

First she flipped through Gilbert's senate calendar, hoping to find notes of meetings with anyone from WRVH. Nancy felt her heart skip a beat. On the previous Wednesday, Gilbert had scheduled a meeting with Marilyn Morgan! Nancy jotted down the time and location of the meeting—a restaurant called the Proud Bird in River Heights.

Next Nancy's glance fell on Steve Gilbert's pen

cup. One of the pens in the cup looked familiar, so she picked it up. It was a novelty pen with a truck that slid back and forth when you shook it—just like the one she had discovered in the tape feed booth.

Nancy peered closely at the pen. The lettering on this one was clearly legible: KSM Express.

"Bingo!" she whispered softly. KSM Express was on the top of Hal's list of companies that were bribing Steve Gilbert!

She quickly copied the address of the company onto a slip of paper. Then she put the pen back into the cup and listened at the door. Hearing nothing, she stepped out of the office into the waiting room.

"Why, Nancy Drew," Nancy heard a voice announce. "We meet again!"

Nancy whirled to see the triumphant face of Brenda Carlton, who was sitting in a wing chair next to the aide's desk. "You'd better give me the whole story this time," Brenda continued acidly, "or I'll tell Steve Gilbert all about your little breaking and entering adventure!"

Chapter

Eight

NANCY STARED AT BRENDA, a feeling of dread welling up inside her. Brenda certainly had a way of showing up at the worst possible times!

"I don't suppose it matters now, but how did you know I was here?" Nancy asked.

Brenda regarded her with a self-satisfied air. "You're not the only one who can play detective, Nancy. I had a hunch you were doing more than 'interning' at Channel Nine, so I waited near your house and followed you this morning," she said. "Now, what's the scoop? Why are you so interested in Steve Gilbert?"

Nancy sighed. She knew she'd have to placate Brenda somehow—she couldn't afford to have her cover blown.

"Let's get out of here before someone finds us," Nancy said, motioning for Brenda to follow her. As they stepped into the corridor, the two girls almost bumped into Steve Gilbert's aide, who was returning to the office. Fortunately, the aide was looking down at some papers in his hands. He didn't notice the two girls.

"Now, Nancy, I want to know *exactly* what you've got up your sleeve," Brenda demanded after they ducked into an empty rest room.

Without mentioning the threats that had been made against Hal Taylor, Nancy admitted that she was working on a case at WRVH. "I'm helping Hal work on a story involving Steve Gilbert, but we haven't come up with anything worthwhile yet. Actually, I think his story is going to be a bust," Nancy lied. "So there's nothing I can tell you at this point."

Brenda looked skeptical. "Sounds like Hal Taylor's trying to dig up some dirt on Steve Gilbert." She pulled a folded newspaper from her purse and waved it in Nancy's face. Gilbert's face was on the front page.

"This is the first installment of my series on Steve Gilbert as an up-and-coming political figure," Brenda said. "I can use whatever you find out about him for my next article. So you'd better keep me informed—or I'll tell him everything."

Brenda's tone made Nancy grit her teeth, but she forced a pleasant smile. "I'll let you know as soon as *I* know anything," she promised. Then she escaped down the hallway.

According to their prearranged plan, Nancy met Bess back at the parking lot.

"You did a great job distracting Gilbert's aide, Bess," Nancy told her friend. "Mata Hari couldn't have worked it any better."

Bess batted her eyes with a mock femme fatale look. "I didn't mind that assignment one bit. That guy was so cute!" she said. "How about you? Did you manage to find any clues in Gilbert's office?"

"Yes, but unfortunately I managed to find Brenda Carlton as well."

"Oh, no," Bess groaned. "What happened?"

Nancy quickly told her about the encounter. "I think I put her off for the moment, though," she finished. "The good news is that I found out from Gilbert's desk calendar that Marilyn Morgan had an appointment with him last week. *And* I found another clue."

She told Bess about the novelty pen in the pen cup that matched the one she'd found in the tape booth at the station. "With a little more investigation, I may be able to connect Gilbert and Marilyn to the threats against Hal."

"Do you think Gilbert dropped the pen at the station?" Bess asked as the two girls climbed into Nancy's Mustang.

Nancy shook her head. "It's unlikely that he could have gotten into the station. Finding this pen just backs up my theory that Gilbert must have an accomplice at WRVH."

"Marilyn?" Bess guessed, raising an eyebrow.

"It's possible," Nancy replied. "But I need to find more evidence before I can accuse her of being behind the attacks against Hal."

Nancy snapped on her seat belt, then began the drive back to River Heights. "The first thing I want to do when we get back is check out the company whose name was on that pen," Nancy said as she nosed the car onto the highway. "It's called KSM Express. I think it's some kind of trucking company."

"How does KSM Express tie in to the threats against Hal?" Bess asked.

"I know from Hal that KSM Express is one of the companies that has supposedly been bribing Gilbert," she answered. "Since Hal's going to air the bribery story on Monday, that gives both Gilbert and this company a strong motive to scare him off."

Bess nodded thoughtfully. "So you think Marilyn is the one who left the pen in the feed booth."

"If Marilyn is in league with Gilbert, then it's possible that she could be involved with KSM as well," she said slowly. "On the other hand, I can't forget about Gary Krieger."

Nancy filled Bess in on the reporter's suspicious behavior the day before. "There's still a possibility that he could be behind the threats. I just have to keep looking until I find some hard evidence to connect him or Marilyn to the attacks." She pressed her lips together thoughtfully. "I just hope I can prove who's

71

behind this before there's another incident. That fire in Hal's office yesterday proved that the situation is becoming really dangerous for him."

Nancy spotted a tiny roadside restaurant and pulled into the parking lot. "Let's stop here for lunch," she suggested. "I don't know about you, but all this sleuthing has made me hungry."

Nancy and Bess devoured a delicious lunch of soup and apple fritters. Then they continued their drive back to River Heights. They drove past the River Heights airport on their way to find KSM Express, which was located in an industrial area on the east side of town.

The company lay at the end of a road near some railroad tracks. The company's large parking lot was crowded with eighteen-wheel trucks.

Bess held her nose as one of the huge trucks pulled past them, belching out a cloud of thick black exhaust from its smokestack. "Yuck!" she cried. "This definitely isn't the most glamorous assignment we've ever been on."

"I'm afraid trucking companies tend to be short on glamour, as a rule," Nancy said with a laugh.

She pulled her Mustang into the parking lot, and she and Bess got out and went to the double glass doors of KSM Express. A receptionist looked up from her desk.

"May I help you?" she asked pleasantly.

"Yes," Nancy said, thinking fast. She glanced at a stack of business cards in a holder on the desk. The top card read: KSM Express. Kurt Milhaus, President. "I have an appointment to see Kurt Milhaus," Nancy finished smoothly.

The receptionist looked confused as she checked a calendar on her desk. "I'm afraid Mr. Milhaus just stepped out of the office for a minute. I don't seem to have a record of an appointment for him. You said your name was . . . ?"

"Nancy Drew and Bess Marvin," Nancy supplied.

"I'm so sorry," the receptionist told her. "I can set up an appointment with him for Monday, if you like."

Nancy shot Bess a quick look, then said, "We'll just wait for him, if you don't mind."

"Well . . ." The receptionist seemed as if she were about to object, but Bess spoke up before she could.

"Do you have a ladies' room we could use while we're waiting?" Bess asked.

The receptionist looked annoyed, but she pointed to a doorway at the end of the hall. "It's through that door and down to your right," she said.

"Good job, Bess," Nancy whispered as they hurried down the corridor. Looking ahead, she spotted a door at the end of the long hallway. "Let's try that door," she said. "Maybe it leads to

Kurt Milhaus's office. He's the president of the company."

The two girls stepped through the door and were surprised to find themselves outside on a vast loading dock. At the far end of the dock, they could see a crew of workers loading crates into the back of a tractor-trailer truck. The entire warehouse seemed to vibrate with the rumbling of heavy machinery and the shouts of the workers. No one seemed to notice Nancy and Bess. They stood in the doorway and quickly surveyed the scene.

"The trucking business seems like such a plain-Jane kind of operation," Bess whispered. "Why would a company like this want to bribe a politician?"

Nancy pointed to the truck that the workers were loading. "Hal told me that Milhaus wants to avoid complying with safety laws and pollution controls," she said. "So he bribed Gilbert to write exemptions into the legislation."

"So that's why I got a lungful of black smoke as we drove in here!" Bess said indignantly.

Nancy nodded. "I still want to find Milhaus's office," she said. "Let's see if we can locate it before the receptionist realizes we've disappeared."

Nancy and Bess skirted around some huge packing barrels, heading back toward the door to the main office. Suddenly, Nancy heard a low rumbling behind her, followed by a screech of brakes.

She whirled around and looked up in horror. A forklift, loaded with heavy wooden boxes, was bearing down on her and Bess. In the next instant, the forklift slammed to a halt.

Nancy gasped as the crates tumbled from the forklift, heading straight for her and Bess!

Chapter

Nine

"Look out, Bess!" Nancy cried, shoving her away from the wall of falling boxes.

Nancy barely managed to leap aside herself and fell hard on the concrete floor. A split second later one of the crates crashed onto the spot where she had just been standing. The heavy wooden crate splintered apart with a sickening crack.

"Nancy, are you all right?" Bess's face was white with shock as she came over to help Nancy to her feet.

"I'm okay, but I can't say the same for my panty hose," she joked, brushing some dirt off her torn stockings.

The forklift driver, who was wearing a

foreman's hard hat, leapt off his vehicle. "What are you girls doing in this area!" he shouted.

"We took a wrong turn," Nancy replied, half-truthfully.

"Accidents happen when you go snooping around where you don't belong," the foreman continued angrily. "I'll bet that's *your* Mustang I saw outside with the Channel Nine sticker on it! We don't want any more reporters poking around here!"

He certainly wasn't acting apologetic! Nancy thought. In fact, it was almost as if he had deliberately tried to run them down with the forklift.

"But of course it *was* an accident," another voice smoothly interrupted the foreman's tirade. "Right, Merrick?"

Nancy turned to see a well-dressed business-man who looked about twenty-five years old. He was standing in a doorway to the office building and was carrying a leather attaché case.

"Right, Mr. Milhaus. Of course I didn't see them," the foreman said, tugging at his hard hat.

"You can go tell the crew to clean up this mess," Kurt Milhaus told Merrick, gesturing toward the heap of broken crates.

"Yes, sir," the man replied. He glared over his shoulder at Nancy and Bess as he headed toward the back of the warehouse.

Milhaus turned to face the two girls. "I'm sorry about Merrick's bad manners. He tends to be a hot-under-the-collar type, but he's a good fore-man. I hope neither of you was hurt."

Bess, who still appeared to be in shock, said nothing. Nancy shook her head. "We're all right, except for getting quite a scare."

Milhaus motioned for them to follow as he opened the door to the main office building. "This area is off limits to visitors for safety reasons just like this," he explained. "The receptionist told me you had gone to the ladies' room. How did you wind up out here?"

"We must have taken a wrong turn," Nancy said.

Milhaus nodded thoughtfully. "I guess that could happen to anybody," he said slowly. "You said you had an appointment?"

"Well, we didn't exactly have an *appointment*," Bess said, springing back to life. She gave Kurt Milhaus her most appealing smile. "We were just hoping you might be able to make time to see us."

Milhaus chuckled as he glanced from Bess to Nancy. "I have a meeting in a few minutes, but I guess I can squeeze in the time for two attractive young ladies."

Good going, Bess, Nancy thought. She followed Kurt Milhaus down a second hallway and into his private office. She and Bess sat down in the office's green leather chairs, while Mr. Milhaus leaned casually against his desk. Above the desk was a picture of him with Steve Gilbert at some sort of ribbon-cutting ceremony.

"Now, what did you want to see me about?" Milhaus asked pleasantly.

"I'm working as an intern at Channel Nine,"

Nancy explained. "We're just doing some fact-checking on a story about trucking deregulation."

"Fact-checking, huh?" Kurt Milhaus leaned back in his chair and clucked his tongue reprovingly. "Look, I don't hold this against you personally, but I had a very unpleasant interview with one of your reporters, Hal Taylor, about a month ago. He implied all sorts of slanderous things about this company and about me in particular. I'm prepared to sue the station if he broadcasts any of those lies. There's a 'fact' that you can tell him for me."

"I can understand why you'd be upset," Nancy said sympathetically. She spotted a pen cup on Mr. Milhaus's desk. Taking out her reporter's notebook, she pretended to search for a pen. "I'm sorry, I can't find a pen. May I borrow one of yours, Mr. Milhaus? I just want to take a few notes for Hal."

The man nodded and handed her a novelty pen with the KSM company name on it. It was exactly the same as the one she had found at the station and in Steve Gilbert's office.

"This is so cute!" Nancy gushed, turning the pen over so that the truck ran back and forth. "It even has your company name on it."

Smiling pleasantly, Mr. Milhaus said, "We had those custom-made to give to friends and clients. Handing out little gifts like that is good for business."

I'm sure it is, Nancy thought, thinking of the cash "gifts" that Kurt Milhaus had given to Steve

Gilbert. She smiled brightly and said, "I'm sure I saw one of these pens just the other day, over at Channel Nine. Does one of your friends work there?"

Milhaus's face reddened slightly. "Certainly not," he replied. Nancy thought she could detect a slight nervousness in his voice. "These pens—we hand out so many. They could end up anywhere, I suppose."

Nancy found herself studying the businessman's face. She was certain that she had never met him before, yet there was something oddly familiar about his appearance. She couldn't shake the feeling that she had run into him before.

"I have to get to my other appointment," Mr. Milhaus said, checking his watch. Nancy and Bess rose, and he escorted them to the door. "I hope you can convince Hal not to run that interview he shot here the other day. He's way off base."

"I'm sure he's only interested in telling the truth," Nancy replied carefully.

For just a moment, the mask of congeniality dropped away from Kurt Milhaus's face. A hard, calculating look came into his eyes. Then the look was gone, and he smiled. "That's good," he said evenly. "Tell Hal we'll meet again soon."

Nancy was taken aback by the man's tone. Was that a threat? She resolved to ask Hal about the exact nature of his dealings with Kurt Milhaus when she returned to the station.

* * * *

"What do you think, Nancy?" Bess asked as the two girls got back into Nancy's Mustang.

Nancy turned on the ignition. "I think Kurt Milhaus is pretty nervous about Hal's upcoming story, but that doesn't prove he's behind the attacks," she said, backing out of the parking lot.

"I got the feeling that the foreman was deliberately trying to scare us—or worse," Bess said with a shiver.

"They certainly aren't fans of Channel Nine," Nancy said. "Milhaus obviously knows that Hal is implicating him in his story. That could explain the foreman's reaction."

Her blue eyes narrowed thoughtfully as she headed toward downtown River Heights. "So far the only tie-in I have between Milhaus and the attacks is that KSM Express pen I found in the tape booth—and that isn't much to go on," she admitted. "But there's something else that bothers me about Milhaus."

"What is it?" Bess asked.

"I'm not exactly sure—it's something about his face, I think," Nancy answered. "He looks very familiar to me."

"That's odd. Is there any way you two could have met or seen each other before today?"

Nancy shook her head. "No. I have a good memory for faces. With those bushy black eyebrows of his, I know I would have recognized him if I'd ever seen him before. So I can't understand why I have this eerie feeling that we've met."

Bess opened her purse and pulled out a compact. "Maybe you're having déjà vu?"

"Maybe," Nancy said. "But I can't help feeling that if I could figure out why he looks so familiar, it would help solve this case."

Seeing a convenience store just beyond a highway overpass, Nancy signaled, then pulled her car into the parking lot. She stopped next to a pay phone outside the store. "I'm just going to call Mr. Liski to check up on Hal and let him know I'm heading back," she told Bess. "I'll drop you at the restaurant on the way so you won't be late for work."

"Okay," Bess said, sighing dramatically. "I guess I'll just have to wait another day for my big chance to meet Hal Taylor."

Nancy laughed. "Believe me. As long as Marilyn Morgan is on the scene, you're better off staying miles away from him!"

She opened her door and started to get out. All of a sudden, the quiet afternoon was shattered by the shrill blast of a truck's air horn. Nancy barely had time to turn around when she heard the sickening sound of metal crashing against metal.

"Get down, Bess!" Nancy cried, ducking back inside the car. The next thing she knew, the car was rocked by a powerful explosion!

Chapter

Ten

Look over there, Bess!" Nancy pointed toward the nearby highway overpass.

Two huge trucks had crashed into each other on top of the bridge. One of them, a tanker truck, was engulfed in flames. The other truck had smashed through the road barrier. It was dangling precariously over the edge of the bridge.

"Wh-what happened?" Bess tentatively raised her head to look where Nancy was pointing. "Oh, no!" she cried. "Someone is trapped inside that truck!"

Nancy could see the driver waving frantically. "It could fall over the edge any second," she said tensely. "We've got to call for help!"

She was relieved to see a police car parked outside the convenience store. The officer inside must have heard the crash, too, because he came racing out, a half-eaten doughnut in his hand. He immediately got into his car and started talking on his police radio. Nancy and Bess assumed he was summoning emergency vehicles. Then he gunned the motor of the patrol car and raced out of the parking lot.

Nancy leapt out of her car, digging in her purse for some change. "I'm telephoning the station," she told Bess. "This is the sort of thing they need to know about right away."

She sprinted to the pay phone and dialed the station's number. When she described the crash to a newsroom assistant, Otto Liski quickly came on the line.

"What have you got?" he asked in his no-nonsense style.

Already, Nancy could see fire trucks and ambulances pulling up to the crash scene. A column of smoke was rising from the tanker truck. Crews were attaching steel wires to the other truck in an effort to keep it from falling off the bridge. She described the scene and the explosion to the producer.

Mr. Liski put Nancy on hold briefly, then came back on the line. "Nancy, all our other reporters are on assignment a good ways from that area," he said. "I know this isn't part of your case," he added quietly, "but I want you to go over there and gather the facts about what happened. Krieger's on his way, but we may need the information sooner for our afternoon broadcast —we go on the air in less than fifteen minutes."

"No problem," Nancy replied. "I'll get right on it."

"One of our camera trucks is around the corner from you, getting a weather shot, so I raised the crew over the two-way radio and told them to meet you," Liski added. "When they get there, direct them to take pictures of whatever looks important. We'll need all the footage they can muster, and *quickly.*"

Nancy hung up and jumped back into the Mustang.

"What do they want you to do?" Bess asked.

"They need me to work as a reporter, at least until a real one shows up," Nancy said as she grabbed her pen and reporter's notebook. "You'd better stay here, though. It could be dangerous."

"Don't worry—I'm happy to watch from a safe distance," Bess replied. She looked nervously back at the two trucks, which were shrouded in smoke and flames. "Be careful, Nancy."

Nancy jogged over to the crash site, taking care to stay out of the way of the emergency vehicles that were beginning to cluster on the scene. Paramedics and fire fighters had already rescued the driver of the burning tanker truck. So far they'd been unable to reach the other driver, though, who was still trapped in the cab of his truck, which was dangling off the edge of the bridge.

No one objected to Nancy's presence at the emergency scene—they were too busy concentrating on the task at hand. She found a police sergeant who seemed to be directing the emergency operations.

"I'm with Channel Nine news," Nancy said, showing her ID and opening her reporter's notebook. "Can you tell me what happened here?"

"It looks like one of the drivers fell asleep at the wheel and crashed into the other truck," the sergeant replied. "It turns out he'd been driving for seventeen hours without stopping. He just passed out."

"The state legislature just dropped some legislation that would have prevented truck drivers from working such long hours," Nancy commented angrily as she made her notes. "That legislation would have prevented accidents like this."

The police sergeant nodded. "If the public knew about the dangers of overtired drivers, there'd be a lot *more* safety regulations, I can tell you."

Nancy looked up and saw the Channel 9 news van pulling into view. Marcus Snipes and Danny McAnliss jumped out of the van. Without a word, Danny quickly assembled his camera pack and began shooting the scene.

"Hi, Nancy," Marcus greeted her, looking at the dangling truck. "Wow! Looks like we've got a big story here."

"Liski wants this to go on right away," Nancy told Danny and Marcus. "We'll need your pictures of the crash scene, Danny. Marcus and I can interview the police sergeant I was talking to earlier, so we'll have him on tape. Let me call Liski again now and see what else we should do."

Mr. Liski spoke rapidly when Nancy called him over the van's two-way radio. "Nancy, we're going on the air shortly, and I heard that the other stations have their crews on the way to the scene," he said, his words tense. As he spoke, Nancy spotted a news van from a rival station coming up the road toward the crash scene. "I've assigned Krieger, but he's still fifteen minutes away. Do you think you could handle a live shot?"

A live shot! Nancy thought. That meant she herself would appear on camera, describing the disaster as it happened for thousands of Channel 9 viewers.

"I'll do my best," she replied. She tried to sound calm despite the butterflies in her stomach. "How long do you need me to speak on camera?"

"About a minute and thirty seconds," came Liski's reply. "You'll open with a description of the explosion and crash. Then Hal will ask you a couple of questions from the anchor desk."

"No problem, Mr. Liski," Nancy replied, wishing she were really that confident.

"Great. I'll have Danny set up the dish for a live shot," Mr. Liski said, referring to the small satellite dish that sat on top of the news van. He quickly described the way the dish worked—it would transmit live pictures of the scene to the station's remote broadcast tower. From there, the tower would beam the pictures into thousands of homes.

Nancy handed the phone to Danny, then quickly got to work. She interviewed the police sergeant again, this time with Marcus taping them.

"Great interview, Nancy," Marcus said after they wrapped up the filming and were headed back to the van. "I can already tell you're a natural reporter. This will be a great debut for your career, if you want one."

"Thanks," Nancy said sincerely. She appreciated the compliment, even though she had no intention of taking up reporting.

While Danny set up his camera and angled the satellite dish for the live shot, which would be aired together with the taped report, Nancy walked back to her car to make some notes about what she would say in front of the camera.

"What's happening?" Bess asked anxiously.

"Bess, I need to borrow your compact mirror," Nancy said. "I have to go on the air in a minute." She quickly retied the belt of her coat. "Thank goodness we went out and bought all those new clothes!"

"You're going on *live* TV?" Bess exclaimed. "Nan, that's so exciting!"

Nancy was too nervous to answer. She quickly ran a comb through her hair and dabbed on some lipstick.

"Here, let a professional do it," Bess said. She opened her purse and pulled out a complete makeup and hair kit, including a miniature can of hairspray.

"We don't have time for that," Nancy protested, but Bess ignored her objection.

"You have to make up for the camera—it washes out all the natural color," she said firmly, dusting Nancy's face with some rose blusher.

Nancy grinned. "I can't believe you drag around all those cosmetics, Bess."

"My motto is be prepared—you never know when you might have to look right for *Mr.* Right," Bess replied. "Don't smile, Nan—you'll mess up the eyeliner."

When Bess had finished applying the last spritz of hairspray, Nancy saw Danny signaling her from the news van. "Come on and watch, Bess," she said as she sprinted toward the camera setup.

Marcus gave Nancy a tiny earpiece so that she could listen to what was being said at the station.

"We're almost ready to go on the air," Nancy heard the producer explain over the earpiece. "You'll be able to hear what the anchors are saying, but obviously you won't be able to see them. Look directly into the camera when you're talking. Good luck, kid."

"Thanks, Mr. Liski," Nancy said, and took a deep breath.

"Forty seconds to air," Marcus announced.

Nancy picked up the microphone and cleared her throat. She forced herself to relax—this was no time for stage fright!

"Five seconds," Marcus said, then gave Nancy her cue to speak.

Nancy looked directly into the camera. "We're at the scene of a spectacular collision between two huge tanker trucks on Highway Forty-two at Isis Road," Nancy began. She briefly summed up the basic facts of the crash, including the fire and rescue efforts. Then there was a pause as the tape of Nancy's interview with the police sergeant was played over the air. When the tape finished, Hal Taylor came on the line.

"Do we know yet what caused the crash?" he asked Nancy.

"Police officials say the crash was caused by an overtired truck driver who fell asleep at the wheel," she explained. "This crash comes on the heels of the state senate's decision to scuttle legislation that would have prevented drivers from working double shifts."

Nancy listened as Hal thanked her for her report. Then Danny signaled that they were off the air. Otto Liski's voice came over the line. "Good job, Nancy! You sounded like a real pro," he said. "I liked the way you made the tie-in to inaction by the state legislature. And we beat the competition on this story by at least fifteen minutes, thanks to you and the crew."

Nancy quickly began unfastening her microphone gear. Now that her reporting job was done, she was eager to get back to the station and pursue her investigation into the threats against Hal.

She watched as a tiny green sports car came racing up at breakneck speed. It threw up a spurt of gravel and dust as it screeched to a halt in front

of the news van. Gary Krieger jumped out of the car and rushed up to Danny.

"What've you got here?" he demanded. "An explosion?"

"You'd better ask *her,*" Danny said, nodding toward Nancy. "She already did all the interviews—and the live shot."

"What?" Gary's face reddened with rage. "Liski *knew* I was on my way! Why didn't he wait until I got here?"

"He just asked me to fill in temporarily so that we could lead the four o'clock news with the crash story," Nancy explained. She held out her notes to Gary. "I'll be glad to fill you in on what happened."

Glaring at her, he knocked the notebook out of her hand. "Don't think you're going to launch your broadcasting career on *my* beat," he said with an ugly snarl. "You'd better stay out of my way, Nancy—or *else!*"

Chapter

Eleven

NANCY MET Gary's glare without blinking.

"Or else *what?*" she retorted. "Are you threatening me because you lost an assignment—just like you've been threatening Hal Taylor?"

Nancy hoped that Gary's anger would provoke him into revealing if he was connected with the attacks against Hal. To her surprise, all of the rage drained from the man's face. He looked stunned for a moment, then his expression became confused.

"You think *I'm* behind the attacks on Hal?" he asked incredulously. "Look, maybe I don't respect the guy, but I'd never actually hurt him."

"It's hard for me to believe that, since you just threatened me," Nancy replied hotly. "For in-

stance, it would have been very easy for you to have set that fire in Hal's office, considering your background as a fire fighter. *And* you were wearing a jacket like the one Clay Jurgenson saw right around the time of the fire."

Gary looked defensive. "I didn't set that fire— *or* play that threatening tape the other night," he insisted. He looked down at the ground and poked at the dirt with his toe. "I admit I fly off the handle sometimes," he said. "But basically I'm pretty harmless. I always push hard because that's what it takes to be a good reporter. Anyway, I'm sorry if I offended you, Nancy." He held out his hand toward her. "Truce?"

Despite her lingering suspicions about him, Nancy shook his hand. "No harm done," she said.

The reporter picked up her notebook from the ground and dusted it off. "Danny, you did a bang-up job on that live shot. Congratulations. Thanks for the notes. I'll review them for my report."

Bess jumped out of the van, where she'd been chatting with Marcus. "I watched your whole report on the monitor inside the van," she said, hurrying over to Nancy. "It looked great! If you keep this up you'll become a celebrity."

"Believe me, Bess, I don't want to be famous," Nancy said, shaking her head wryly. "I'd never be able to do undercover work again."

It was beginning to snow lightly as Nancy and Bess drove to the restaurant where Bess worked.

"To think that the state senate wouldn't pass a

law that could have prevented that accident," Bess said angrily. "It makes me realize how important it is that Hal's story go on the air, despite whoever wants to stop him."

"Gary Krieger's still on my list of suspects," Nancy said. She described the way he had threatened her following the live shot. "I haven't decided whether he's just an excitable type or really dangerous."

Ten minutes later, Nancy dropped Bess off at the restaurant. "What are your plans for tonight?" Bess asked, opening the passenger door.

"Tonight is strictly R and R," Nancy replied. "Ned has a long weekend break, so he's coming home from Emerson. Dad and Hannah are both going to be out, so I've planned an old-fashioned evening by the fireplace. We're going to roast marshmallows."

"If I know you and Ned, marshmallows aren't the *only* things that'll get heated up," Bess teased.

Nancy blushed. "I have to admit it'll be great to see him again," she said.

The two girls said goodbye, then Nancy put the car into gear.

Nancy was watching TV in the living room later that evening, when she heard the doorbell ring. She opened the door eagerly to find Ned standing there.

"Hi, there, Drew," Ned said softly, his dark eyes shining as they swept over her.

"Hey, Nickerson," she replied. She melted into his arms for a long, lingering kiss. Ned looked more handsome than ever, Nancy thought. A light bronze glow touched his cheeks, and he was wearing an ivory fisherman's sweater that brought out the warmth of his brown eyes.

Ned raised his arm to show Nancy the bag of nuts he was clutching in his fist. "You know the old song about roasting chestnuts and an open fire?" he said. "Well, that's what I've planned for us tonight."

"I always wanted to roast chestnuts with a handsome guy. I guess you'll have to do, though," Nancy teased.

Ned's strong arms slipped around her waist. Nancy leaned against him, enjoying the feel of his sweater's rough weave against her cheek.

"Where are your dad and Hannah?" Ned asked.

"Dad has a business dinner, and Hannah's visiting her sister for a few days," Nancy replied. "So we have the place to ourselves."

Soon they were lounging in front of a roaring fire in the living room. Nancy leaned back against a big pile of pillows, with Ned's head resting on her lap. She plucked two marshmallows from a glass bowl and stuck them onto a long wooden stick.

"I'll let you do the cooking," Ned murmured lazily. "I like my marshmallows burned black on the outside and gooey inside."

"And these were going to be perfect golden brown specimens." Nancy laughed. "Here goes," she announced, holding the marshmallows directly over the flame. When the marshmallows had turned completely black, Ned took one off the stick and popped it into his mouth.

"Umm," he said, licking his fingers. "Nobody burns 'em like you, Nancy," he said teasingly. After they had devoured numerous marshmallows and chestnuts, Nancy reached for the television remote control.

"I hate to break the mood," she said, "but I have to watch Hal Taylor on the late news to make sure everything goes okay."

"What's going on at Channel Nine, anyway?" Ned asked. Nancy briefly described the incidents at the station. When she told him about the bribes that Gilbert had been accepting, Ned shook his head.

"Let me know if there's anything I can do to help you on this case," he said. "From what you're saying, this Gilbert character sounds like a real sleazeball."

"Thanks, Ned," Nancy said. "I'll let you know if I need any help."

When Hal finished the late news, Nancy clicked off the program. "Thank goodness everything went smoothly," she said.

Ned reached up and stroked Nancy's hair. "Now tell me, what's the *real* scoop at Channel Nine?" he asked. "Are there any tall, dark, and handsome news reporters I have to watch out for?"

Nancy thought about her experience with the world of reporters over the past couple of days. Her initial attraction to Hal Taylor had quickly faded away once she started investigating the case. Despite his good looks, there was something very self-centered about the anchorman, she realized. She could truthfully say that Ned had no competition at Channel 9.

Leaning over, she kissed the tip of Ned's nose. "Don't you know you're the only tall, dark, and handsome guy who matters to me?" she said softly.

Ned responded by curling a hand gently around Nancy's neck and drawing her head toward his. Their lips met in a long, sizzling kiss, and Nancy's heart soared.

The next morning, Nancy got up before the alarm went off. She was determined to follow up on the leads she had developed the day before, including Marilyn Morgan's possible involvement with Steve Gilbert.

The newsroom was practically deserted when Nancy arrived, but she knew it would be bustling soon. Even though it was Saturday, the newsroom was busy seven days a week.

Otto Liski was one of the few people around, Nancy saw. He was already working at his desk. "Don't you ever sleep?" she asked him lightly, stopping in his office doorway.

Mr. Liski looked up from the sheaf of wire service copy he was marking and shook his head ruefully. "I'm a typical news producer—we live on deadlines, caffeine, and nervous energy," he said with a smile. "Television is a twenty-four-hour-a-day business, and after a while it takes over your life." He glanced curiously at Nancy. "So how's the investigation coming?" he asked.

Nancy quickly filled him in on her experience at KSM Express. She described her suspicions about Kurt Milhaus and showed him the pen she had found in the station's tape booth.

"I've linked this pen to KSM Express," she said. "Milhaus seemed pretty nervous when I told him I found it at the station."

"Then it's likely that he could be working with Gilbert. He must know that he would be exposed in Hal's story as well," Liski commented.

Nancy nodded. "Evidently Hal's interview with Milhaus was pretty stormy, so he probably knows the gist of what Hal will be reporting on the air."

Mr. Liski took the pen from Nancy and examined it. "So whoever dropped this in the tape booth must have a connection to Milhaus. But who is it?"

"I found out that Marilyn Morgan had a meeting with Gilbert last Wednesday," Nancy said.

"Marilyn met with Gilbert!" Liski sounded shocked. "Why would she do that?"

Nancy took a deep breath. "It makes perfect sense if she's the person who is collaborating with Gilbert," she explained.

"It's possible there's some reasonable explanation for her meeting with him," the producer said slowly, handing the pen back to Nancy. "But we'll have to confront her with your discovery—and soon."

"I'd like to do a little more digging before we make any accusations," Nancy said. "Meanwhile, has the arson squad turned up anything?"

"They confirmed what you suspected. The fire was set by someone who used lighter fluid," Liski replied. He wearily rubbed his forehead. "I just can't believe that Marilyn would be behind it." He looked up at Nancy. "What do you have planned for today?"

"I'd like to review any of your old news tapes that have to do with Steve Gilbert," Nancy said. "Do you have a library where you store the old tapes?"

Otto Liski nodded and jumped to his feet. "We call our tape library the morgue because it's where we put dead news stories," he said. "But I'm warning you—it would take weeks to sift through all those hours of tape."

He led Nancy to a storage room that was crammed floor to ceiling with tapes. They were arranged by subject. After showing her how to view the tapes, Liski said, "Good luck," and then left.

Several hours later, Nancy had finished viewing a stack of tapes in one of the editing booths. She had to plow through hundreds of stories about the state legislature to find anything remotely linked to Steve Gilbert. Most of the stories were routine committee-meeting reports, she was frustrated to discover.

She was beginning to think she would never find anything useful, when she popped the last tape into the machine. She fast-forwarded to the beginning of the story, which was about trucking deregulation. Kurt Milhaus was standing on the podium beside Steve Gilbert. Once again, Nancy was struck by how familiar Milhaus's face looked.

At the end of the story, there were a few seconds of outtake footage—stray shots that weren't part of the story but were tacked on by a videotape editor in case they were needed for a longer version of the story. In the outtakes, Nancy could see Gilbert and Milhaus huddling in a corner of the conference room during a break in the meeting. She saw Milhaus hand Gilbert something.

Whoa! Nancy's mind screamed. What was that? After rewinding the tape, she played that section over again. Even at extra slow speed, she could barely make out a white envelope that Milhaus passed to Gilbert. The politician stuffed the envelope into his jacket pocket.

Could Steve Gilbert have been reckless enough to accept a bribe at a public meeting? Nancy wondered. Apparently he had been unaware that the camera was turned on.

Nancy returned all the tapes to the morgue except for the one with Kurt Milhaus in it. Tucking the tape under her arm, she headed back to the newsroom to look for Hal. She wanted to ask him whether he'd seen the outtake footage.

By this time it was late morning, and the

newsroom was throbbing with activity. Reporters and camera crews milled about. Otto Liski was posting new assignments on the large chalkboard. Behind him, the sound of a crackling police scanner added to the sense of confusion.

Hal wasn't there, so she headed down the hallway that led to his office. His desk, which had been ruined by the fire, had been replaced and Hal had insisted on remaining in his office, even though it still smelled of smoke. As she approached, she heard loud voices. Through the open door, she saw an enraged Marilyn Morgan standing in front of Hal's desk.

"You *deliberately* tried to embarrass me by bringing her here!" Marilyn shouted, pointing toward a corner of Hal's office. With a start, Nancy noticed that Rita Greenburg was sitting on a chair, looking very uncomfortable. She seemed to be on the verge of tears.

"Be reasonable, Marilyn—" Hal began.

Now Marilyn was the one who burst into tears. By this time, other people had stopped in the hall to gape at Marilyn and Hal. Bill Steghorn brushed past Nancy and went into Hal's office. He put an arm around the anchorwoman's shoulders.

"Let's go back to your office, where you can have some privacy," the engineer said soothingly, leading her down the hallway.

Hal glanced at Rita. "I'm sorry this happened," he told her. Then he looked helplessly at Nancy. "I have to talk to Marilyn, Nancy. Could you . . . ?"

101

"I'll take care of Rita," Nancy offered. Not that she had much choice—Hal was already striding down the hall after Marilyn.

Rita grabbed her coat, and Nancy walked her out to the parking lot. When they reached her car, Rita dabbed at her eyes with a handkerchief.

"So much for my lunch with Hal," she said, sniffling.

"Don't mind Marilyn—" Nancy started to say, but Rita interrupted her.

"I'm not upset because she was yelling. I'm upset because she's *right,*" Rita said sadly. "Hal's still in love with Marilyn. I mean, that's obvious from the way he ran after her just now. I guess I couldn't see that because I had such a crush on him."

"Hal Taylor is definitely crush material," Nancy said gently, remembering her first impression of the anchorman. "So don't blame yourself for getting involved."

"I'm going to call him tonight and tell him we shouldn't go out anymore," Rita said. She managed a rueful smile. "I figure I'd better call it off before he does, if you know what I mean."

Nancy wished her good luck, then said goodbye. She was on her way back to the newsroom, when she ran into Hal in the hallway.

"I was looking for you, Nancy," he said anxiously. "I'm just about to anchor the noon update. How's Rita?"

"As good as could be expected," Nancy replied. She looked around to make sure no one could overhear them, then said, "Hal, it's time we talked seriously about Marilyn. I found out that she had a meeting with Gilbert last week. That means she could very well be behind these attacks."

Hal leaned against the wall, an anguished look on his face. "You'll just have to accept my word that she's not our suspect. I admit she hasn't been acting like it recently, but she's too good a person to do something like setting a fire in my office."

Nancy shook her head. Hal obviously still cared for Marilyn. Nancy just hoped that his feelings weren't blinding him to the fact that she could be trying to harm him.

Checking his watch, Hal added, "I've got to rush if I'm going to make the noon update."

"I'll go with you," Nancy insisted.

Back in the newsroom, a nervous floor director looked relieved to see Hal arrive.

"You're cutting it short today, Hal," she said, clipping a microphone onto his lapel. "Twenty seconds to air."

"No sweat," Hal said, flashing his trademark anchorman's grin. He quickly scanned the script in front of him. When the director threw him a signal, he began reading his noon update.

"Good afternoon from the Channel Nine newsroom," he said to the camera. "Our top story on the four o'clock edition will be a follow-up on yesterday's spectacular collision between two eighteen-wheel trucks on Highway Forty-two. Then at six . . ."

Nancy had taken a seat on a nearby footstool and was watching carefully. Then she heard a low, buzzing noise above Hal's head and looked up. The noise seemed to be coming from somewhere inside the ceiling.

Suddenly, a ceiling panel crashed to the floor, releasing a shower of dust and debris. Nancy gasped and stood up as a thick black wire dropped through the hole in the ceiling. It was crackling with electricity, Nancy realized with a start.

It was a live wire! And it was falling straight toward Hal!

Chapter
Twelve

FOR A SPLIT SECOND, Nancy stood frozen in horror. Then, grabbing the wooden footstool that she had been sitting on, she leapt toward Hal.

She used the stool to push the crackling wire away from him. The force of her momentum caused her to fall hard against him, and the two of them went sprawling in a heap across the floor.

The newsroom erupted into chaos. The floor director shouted through her microphone to the control room, "We've got a hot wire here! Cut the power! Shut it off!"

Otto Liski came running out of his office and grabbed the microphone from the director. He barked another set of commands to the control room. In the next instant, the room was plunged into semidarkness as all power in the station was turned off.

Nancy and Hal struggled awkwardly to their feet. "Are you all right, Hal?" Nancy asked.

"Yes—thanks to you," he replied. He shuddered as he looked at the wire that now hung limply from the ceiling. "Looks like I came close to getting deep-fried," he joked weakly. "I wonder how many volts that thing carries?"

"Enough to roast an elephant," came a deep-voiced reply. Nancy turned to see Bill Steghorn and a technician standing next to Hal's desk. Steghorn used a flashlight to gingerly examine the fallen wire.

"The protective skin is all frayed off this wire," the engineer said indignantly. "This should never have been installed like this. Either someone was incredibly stupid, or—"

"Or it was done deliberately?" Nancy posed the question that was uppermost in everyone's mind. If so, this would be the most serious attack yet.

The engineer looked at Nancy. "Could be," he said thoughtfully.

"But what caused the wire to fall through the ceiling?" Mr. Liski wanted to know.

"Maybe we can find out," said Nancy. "Do you mind if I take a look at the ceiling?" she asked the producer.

"Go ahead," Mr. Liski said. "Just be careful."

Nancy borrowed the technician's flashlight and climbed onto the anchor desk. She shined the beam into the crawl space above the false ceiling of the newsroom and saw a jumble of wires and ropes. Standing on tiptoe, she reached up and carefully felt inside the space. Her hand brushed against something, and a shower of sand fell into the newsroom.

"I found something," Nancy called down to the others. She pulled out a half-empty bag of sand along with a funnel and a tiny mechanical device with a clock on it.

"I'd say a pile of sand caused the ceiling panel to fall," Nancy said. She jumped down from the desk and handed the timer and funnel to Otto Liski.

"What?" he exclaimed. "I don't understand what these are."

Nancy pointed to the funnel. "This funnel and the sandbag were suspended by ropes above the ceiling panel," she explained. "It looks like this timing device was used to control what time the sand would be released through the funnel onto the panel. When enough sand trickled onto the panel . . ."

"It crashed down to the floor," Hal finished slowly, "releasing the live wire."

Nancy nodded, her expression sober. "Someone cut that wire earlier," she said. "And the timer was set to go off at noon. The attacker must have known that you were scheduled to anchor the news update then."

"Someone went to an awful lot of trouble to kill me," Hal said, looking around nervously.

"Someone's head is going to roll for this,"

Steghorn bellowed at the technician. "Who's assigned to work in this area of the overhead circuitry?"

"Clay Jurgenson, I think," the technician replied.

Bill Steghorn shook his head and turned toward Otto Liski. "Jurgenson is one of those temporary workers we've been using since the station had all those layoffs," he explained. "I don't know him too well."

Clay Jurgenson was also the technician who claimed to have seen someone outside Hal's office at the time of the arson fire, Nancy recalled. His job as a temporary worker would be the perfect cover for an outside person trying to attack Hal. He could easily be working for Kurt Milhaus or Steve Gilbert.

As the engineers began repairing the wire, Nancy quietly drew Mr. Liski aside. "I'd like to question Clay Jurgenson right away," she said.

"You and me both," the producer sputtered angrily. "I haven't seen him around today, though. I'll find out whether he's scheduled to work."

After temporarily repairing the wire, Bill Steghorn called for the power to be restored. The lights came back on suddenly, causing Nancy to blink. She looked up as Hal approached Otto Liski and tapped him on the shoulder.

"Otto, don't you think I should go back on the air to explain to the viewers what happened?" Hal asked. "After all, the last image they had was of my being tackled by Nancy—followed by an old rerun of a comedy show. It's hard to decide which is scarier—the tackle or that awful show."

Nancy laughed despite the tension everyone was feeling. Otto Liski gave the okay for Hal to go back on the air, then he went off to find Clay's work schedule. He soon came back, holding a sheet of paper with a grid pattern on it.

"Jurgenson's off work today, according to this schedule," the news producer told Nancy. "And there's no answer at his house, which is listed on Creedmore Street."

"Let's head over there anyway," Nancy said. "Even if we can't question him, maybe we'll find some proof that he's behind the attacks."

Mr. Liski nodded his agreement. "Meet me out in the parking lot," he whispered. "I'll tell anyone who asks that you're heading off to do research on a story."

It was already well past noon, so Nancy grabbed a quick lunch in the station's commissary. On her way to the lobby, she bumped into Marilyn Morgan, who was coming around the corner. The anchorwoman looked shaken.

"I heard what happened in the newsroom. What's happened to Hal?" she asked Nancy anxiously.

Nancy decided to confront the newscaster about her involvement with Steve Gilbert. "You should know what happened to Hal, Marilyn," Nancy said coolly. "After all, you've been working with Steve Gilbert, haven't you?"

THE NANCY DREW FILES

The anchorwoman's eyes widened with fear. "Steve Gilbert? Wh-what do you mean?" she stammered. "What did Gilbert tell you?"

"He didn't tell me anything at all," Nancy retorted. "He didn't have to."

Marilyn glared at Nancy. Without a word, she turned on her heel and stalked away. Nancy didn't have time to go after her. She would have to wait until later to pursue her questions.

Nancy stopped short when she reached the station's lobby. Brenda Carlton was standing there, trying to talk her way past the security guard. She looked furious when she saw Nancy.

"You tried to throw me off the track before," Brenda said accusingly. "The *real* story is that someone is trying to kill Hal Taylor, isn't that right?"

Uh-oh, Nancy thought. She had a big problem on her hands now. If Brenda printed one word of this, the whole story of Hal's predicament and Nancy's investigation would be splashed all over town. And that could destroy all the progress she'd made so far!

"I suspected that something like this was going on," Brenda went on smugly. "So I came over just in time to hear about the wire falling on Hal. And I'm betting it was no accident."

Nancy decided that she had no choice but to level with Brenda—to a point. "You're right about the attacks on Hal," she said. Luckily, no one else was in the reception area to hear her. "Surely you can understand why the station wants to keep it quiet for the time being."

"Why should I cooperate with you and Hal? After all, he's the competition," Brenda said, putting her hands on her hips. "And the fact that someone's going after the town's top anchorman is a dynamite story."

Nancy thought for a moment. It looked as if she would have to bargain with Brenda. "You want a great story, right?" she asked. Brenda nodded emphatically. "All right, then. I promise to give you all the details of my investigation, along with an exclusive interview with Hal Taylor, once this is all over—*if* you promise to give me a couple more days to solve the case."

Brenda looked suspicious, but she finally agreed. "I'll be watching you carefully, though, so don't try to wiggle out of giving me the story," she warned.

Nancy promised, then dashed for the parking lot to meet Otto Liski. Soon they were on their way to find engineer Clay Jurgenson's house, which was located along a row of seedy walk-ups on Creedmore Street.

Nancy parked the car behind a broken-down pickup truck, then she and Liski hurried up to Jurgenson's front door. Mr. Liski knocked, but there was no answer. When he tried the door, it swung open easily. He and Nancy exchanged a glance, then stepped inside.

They found themselves in a living room with a threadbare couch and a table with a television set on it. Nancy saw a kitchen area behind the couch. To the left, a staircase rose up to the second floor. She didn't see or hear anyone.

While Otto Liski looked around downstairs, Nancy climbed the stairs to the second floor, where she found a bedroom and bathroom. In the bedroom, on the engineer's desk, she spotted a desk calendar with a note scribbled on it: KM, 3:00, $25,000.

Could KM stand for Kurt Milhaus? Nancy wondered. The note was entered under the current day's date, which was Saturday. It was just now close to three o'clock, she realized.

She turned as Otto Liski came into the bedroom. "Find anything?" he asked.

Nancy showed him the note on Clay's calendar. "If Milhaus is behind these attacks, there's no question now that he's deadly serious," she said. "He may have paid Jurgenson off to set up the live-wire booby trap." She frowned as she thought of something else. "I'm worried that Milhaus has found out about the tape at Hal's home. I want to head over there and pick it up. Hal told me where he hid it."

"I've been away from the station too long already," Mr. Liski said, frowning. "Believe it or not, I'm trying to take tonight off, so I've got a lot to wrap up this afternoon. I'll call a cab to take me back. But, Nancy, I'm afraid it might be too dangerous for you to go to Hal's alone."

"I'll be fine," Nancy assured him. "But if it makes you feel any better, I'll arrange for my friend Ned Nickerson to meet me over at Hal's."

"Please do," the producer insisted.

Going back down to the kitchen, Nancy used the phone there to call Hal and ask him where she could find his spare key. She also told him about the outtake footage she'd found while searching the tape files earlier that day.

Hal sounded excited by her discovery. "I can't believe I missed that when I was reviewing the old tapes," he said. "We can run it in a slow-motion processor during the discussion of the bribery allegations," he said. "That will really help visualize the story for the audience."

Next Nancy called Ned and asked if he'd mind meeting her at Hal Taylor's.

"Turn down a chance to go on the job with reporter Nancy Drew?" he said in his deep voice. "No way. I'll be there in half an hour to forty-five minutes."

Nancy gave him the address and hung up. After saying goodbye to Liski, she drove across town to Hal's modern split-level house. Ned arrived in his car soon after she had pulled into the circular drive.

"I guess anchors must make pretty big bucks—this is a fancy spread," Ned said as they walked up the path to the front door.

"Everything *seems* quiet," Nancy observed.

Suddenly, she heard a car motor start from somewhere behind the house. Sensing that something was amiss, Nancy quickened her step.

As she raced up the stairs, she could see that the front door was slightly ajar. Nancy threw the door open and looked inside with dismay. Next to her, Ned drew in his breath sharply.

Chairs had been ripped with a knife and overturned, pictures torn from their frames, and debris scattered across the floor. Hal's house had been ransacked!

Chapter
Thirteen

W HAT TORNADO hit this place?" Ned asked soberly, surveying the damage. It was obvious that whoever had done the damage had spent a long time searching for something and was very thorough.

Without saying a word, Nancy bolted through the living room and ran out through Hal's back door. Seeing a service alleyway behind the house, she hurried toward it.

"Wait, Nancy! Where are you going?" Ned called after her.

She was in too much of a hurry to answer. Her head whipped to the left and right as she looked down the empty alley.

"What is it?" Ned asked. He was breathing

115

hard as he came up beside her. "What are you looking for?"

"I heard a car motor start just as we walked up the steps to Hal's house," Nancy replied. "I have a hunch it was probably our vandal." She shook her head in frustration. "If I'd moved faster I might have caught a glimpse of the car."

"Believe me, Nancy, you moved plenty fast," Ned said, bending over and rubbing the back of his calves. "Any faster and we'd have to sign you up for the Olympics."

Nancy was already sprinting back inside Hal's house. She headed for the kitchen and opened a cabinet under the sink. "I hope the tape's still here," she said worriedly.

Ned was right behind her. He looked in the cabinet and shook his head. "Doesn't look like it—all I see are sponges and a bunch of cleaning supplies."

"That's all you're supposed to see," Nancy said. She pulled out a box of soap pads and began fiddling with the box top. With a click, the top of the box slid sideways, revealing a videotape inside.

"It's still here!" she cried triumphantly, pulling the bulky tape from the box with a flourish.

"I can't believe it," Ned said. "That soap box is really some kind of safe?"

Nancy grinned at her boyfriend, who was shaking his head in amazement. "Hal's a nut about unusual gadgets," she explained. "This time his hobby really saved the day."

"That kooky box is even better than a wall

safe," Ned pointed out. "The way this house was torn apart, the burglar probably would have discovered and cracked a regular safe."

Nancy tucked the tape under her arm, and the two of them returned to the living room. "What a mess," Nancy said, looking around. She pulled a pad of paper and pen from her purse. "I'm going to make some notes about the damage for Hal."

"You know, it's spooky the way the attacker struck just before you came to get the tape," Ned observed.

Nancy looked at him thoughtfully. "You may have hit on something, Ned," she said slowly. "I mean, whoever's behind these attacks seems to know our every move." She tried to piece together her thoughts. "Just a little over an hour ago I was talking to Hal and Mr. Liski about coming to get the tape—and then his house was attacked. It's almost as if someone were monitoring our conversations."

Nancy ran outside and checked the spot where Hal had said his spare key would be. As she had expected, the key was missing. "The person knew right where to look," she said, frowning.

"Could anyone have overheard you talking to Hal and that producer, Liski?" Ned asked. "That might explain it."

Nancy shook her head. "Mr. Liski was the only person in Clay's house, and I talked to Hal on the phone," she said. "I guess it *could* have been a coincidence that the attack on Hal's house came right after our conversation, but that doesn't explain how they found out about the key."

She walked into Hal's office, which was off the living room, and looked closely at the pictures that had been ripped from the walls. Most of the pictures that had been torn were publicity photos that showed Hal at work as an anchorman, sometimes alone and sometimes with his co-anchor, Marilyn Morgan.

"There's something odd about the way these photos have been ripped apart," Nancy observed. "Only the ones that include both Hal *and* Marilyn have been torn in half," she said.

Ned picked up one of the torn pictures and peered at it. "Why would someone bother to systematically tear up the photos so that Hal and Marilyn are separated?"

"Maybe because he—or *she*—had more on her mind than just getting the tape," Nancy said excitedly. She gathered up the torn photos of Hal and Marilyn. "I know of only one person with that kind of grudge . . . Marilyn herself."

Ned looked startled. "Marilyn Morgan!" he exclaimed. "But why?"

"She's made it perfectly clear that she'll cross any line when it comes to getting revenge on Hal," Nancy explained.

"Why would she be interested in the bribery tape, though?" Ned asked, still unconvinced.

Nancy reassembled the pieces of one of the pictures of Hal and Marilyn sitting at the anchor desk. In the picture, Hal and Marilyn looked happy—an illusion that was far from the truth, Nancy now realized only too well.

"I know from reading her files that Marilyn is

on the verge of jumping ship to work for another network," she explained. "And she has plenty of motivation to get back at Hal. She may be cooperating with Gilbert to remove Hal from the picture—permanently."

"Wow," Ned said. "It sounds like she definitely has a double motive for revenge—professional *and* romantic jealousy."

Gathering the torn photos into a pile, Nancy said, "I'm going to confront Marilyn with these and remind her that I know about her meeting with Gilbert. Maybe I can startle a confession out of her."

She reached for the phone on Hal's desk. "But first I want to call Hal and tell him what happened. He'll have to call the police, I'm afraid."

"Tell him he'd better call a maid service, too," Ned added, shaking his head in disgust at the destroyed office.

Hal was dismayed by Nancy's news of the vandalizing of his home. "This is getting scary. I can feel this guy breathing down my neck wherever I go," he said. "I can tell he's not going to give up until I'm off the air—or dead."

There was a new note of fear in Hal's voice. For the moment, Nancy decided to withhold her renewed suspicions about Marilyn's role in the attacks. She knew Hal wouldn't believe her unless she had hard evidence. And at the moment, she doubted whether he could handle the information about the torn pictures.

"Hang in there, Hal," she said gently. "I think we're on the verge of solving this case."

"That sounds good to me," Hal said tiredly. "And when we do, I'm heading off for a long vacation."

Nancy said goodbye to Hal and hung up the phone. She and Ned walked out the front door toward their cars.

"Can I see you later tonight?" Ned asked softly. "I have to go back to school to start studying for finals, so it's our last chance until Christmas vacation."

Nancy turned and looked at Ned. "I know I must sound like a nagging parent, but shouldn't you be *studying* tonight if finals start so soon?" she asked.

"I'll be studying my favorite course—Romancing Nancy one-oh-one," Ned protested laughingly.

"Good try, Nickerson." Looping her hands around his neck, she kissed him on the lips. "I don't know if I can get away tonight, but call me just in case," she added in a whisper. "If not, you'd better be prepared to warm up your biology notes."

"Not exactly my idea of a romantic evening," Ned grumbled, but his expression brightened as Nancy melted into his arms in a goodbye kiss.

Nancy's thoughts turned back to the case as she drove back to the TV station. The first thing she wanted to do when she got back was make another copy of Hal's tape for safekeeping. That way they'd be sure to have a tape to use for Hal's upcoming broadcast.

Checking her watch, Nancy saw that it was almost four o'clock. She'd have to hurry in order to be able to talk to Hal before the afternoon news broadcast.

She decided to take a shortcut to save time. Turning off the main road, which skirted a big water reservoir, she headed over to a nearby hill. The local people called the hill Sleeping Giant because it looked like the profile of a man taking a nap on his back. A narrow two-lane road divided the Sleeping Giant between his "head" and "torso."

Nancy climbed the twisting, winding road. It was a difficult road to negotiate, which was the main reason that most people avoided this particular shortcut. She felt almost lightheaded when she reached the top of the hill. The view overlooking the vast reservoir and rolling countryside was breathtaking.

On the other side of the hill's crest, the twisting road suddenly straightened out into a long, steep descent. To the left, there was a flimsy guardrail, then a sheer drop-off that plunged hundreds of feet to the basin below. Several signs were posted near the top of the hill, warning drivers to use a low gear when coming down off the hill. Nancy knew that there had been fatal accidents in the past when a car's brakes had failed, sending it plunging over the cliff.

She moved her Mustang into low gear and started the long drive down. She was still enjoying the scenic view when she was startled by the blast of a truck's air horn directly behind her.

Nancy looked in her rearview mirror, but all she could see were the headlights of an enormous yellow truck. It seemed to have appeared out of thin air! The truck blasted its horn again. The driver seemed to be in a big hurry, Nancy noted nervously.

She shook her head. It was foolish of the driver to want to speed down the mountain. Sticking her hand out the window, Nancy signaled for the driver to pass her.

In the very next instant, she was jolted in her seat by a screaming clash of metal. The huge truck had rammed her bumper! The collision pushed her car into the opposite lane, as she struggled to control it.

Nancy's knuckles were white as she gripped the steering wheel. She hit her horn to warn any oncoming cars, then wrenched the steering wheel to keep control of the car.

She held her breath as the truck's headlights loomed in her rearview mirror again. Had the truck lost its brakes, or had it struck her car deliberately?

Suddenly the truck's air horn blasted again. Then there was another sickening crunch of metal as the truck rammed her car again, harder this time.

The truck was trying to force her car over the edge of the cliff!

Chapter

Fourteen

GRITTING HER TEETH, Nancy tried to wrench the steering wheel away from the cliff edge. It was no use. The Mustang's bumper was caught somehow on the truck's metal grillwork. She was being pushed along helplessly toward a certain death!

In desperation, Nancy pushed her foot down on the accelerator. If she couldn't outmaneuver the truck, maybe she could outrun it. She gunned the motor and felt the Mustang's rear bumper jerk free of the truck. The steering wheel became responsive once again. With great effort, she managed to steer the car back onto the road.

Nancy raced headlong down the mountain. Even at this speed she was just inches ahead of the truck, and it was gathering momentum behind her. She lifted her eyes from the road for a few precious seconds to try to catch a glimpse of the driver in the rearview mirror. The only thing she could see was the truck's front fender, which was decorated with some sort of fancy blue pinstriping.

As she shot down the long, straight hill, Nancy tried to recall what she knew about the road. There were no turnoffs for at least a mile, she knew. She was in a race for her life!

Even without checking the rearview mirror again, she could sense that the truck was gaining on her. Her Mustang's engine surged as she floored the accelerator. In a burst of speed, the speedometer needle leapt forward to seventy, eighty-five, then ninety miles per hour as the two vehicles hurtled down the treacherous road. Nancy knew she was courting disaster by speeding, but the truck looming behind her gave her no choice.

Desperately she tried to remember the last time she had driven this road. She seemed to recall seeing a turnoff near the bottom of the hill. It was barely more than a dirt lane, but it might provide her with a much-needed escape route. The challenge would be making the turn at high speed without losing control and tumbling into a dangerous rollover.

The truck's air horn blasted again, and Nancy knew it was closing in for the third, and possibly fatal, impact. She searched the road ahead of her for signs of the turnoff—there it was!

Nancy eased her foot just slightly off the gas. If she braked too much, the truck would smash her into oblivion. Too little, and she would crash while trying to make the turn.

Her heart leapt into her throat as she felt a sharp jolt. The truck had caught up with her! Taking a deep breath, she wrenched the wheel powerfully to the right.

The Mustang's back end swung out wildly as Nancy veered into the turn. She gasped as the car spun completely around before coming to a stop. She found herself staring at the road she had just left, feeling shaken but unhurt.

Nancy could hear the truck's brakes squeal and gears grind as the driver tried to slow the truck, but it was already well past the turnoff. Then, with a roar of the engine, the truck took off again down the road. Nancy guessed that the driver didn't want to risk her seeing him.

Now that the immediate danger was past, she let out a huge sigh of relief. She felt her hands on the steering wheel begin to tremble slightly.

"Steady, girl," she told herself sternly. "This is no time to fall apart."

Throwing caution to the winds, Nancy slammed her car into gear and peeled out onto the main road. She was determined to catch up with the truck and get its license plate number! She sped down the road for several miles until it fed into a major thoroughfare.

Nancy passed several intersections. The truck could have turned off at any one of the crossroads, but she kept traveling east, following a hunch. KSM Express was located in that direction.

Her pulse quickened as she spotted a yellow truck in the distance. She darted in and out of traffic to catch up with it. Pulling alongside, she saw that it was a moving van. Then she pulled ahead to look at the truck's front bumper—but there was none of the fancy pinstriping she'd seen on the other truck.

"Rats," Nancy muttered, then slowed down.

The truck's driver noticed her staring at his truck. He smiled and gave her a friendly wave. Nancy waved halfheartedly in return. "He probably thinks I'm flirting with him." She groaned and moved into the lane behind him.

She turned off the main road. Her next plan was to look for the truck at KSM Express, but first she wanted to let someone know where she was going in case something happened to her.

Nancy spotted a gas station that had a telephone and stopped to call Ned. She hoped he had gone straight home. He picked up on the fourth ring.

"This is a surprise," he said when he heard her voice. "I was just walking in the door. Couldn't stand being away from me, huh?" he teased. His warm tone quickly turned to concern when she told him what had just happened and that she wanted to search for the pin-striped truck.

"I want to come with you, Nancy," he said.

"You don't have to come," she protested. "I'll be all right."

"I'm going to stick to you like glue for the rest

of the day," he said firmly. "Bess just called here looking for you. I'll pick her up on the way, and we'll both meet you. It's too dangerous to go poking around KSM Express by yourself. Besides, you'll need a lookout, won't you?"

Ned had a point, Nancy had to admit. It would take him a while to make the drive from Mapleton, so she agreed to wait at the gas station for him and Bess to arrive.

After hanging up, she tried to call Otto Liski to tell him what had happened, but the receptionist was unable to locate him for her. He must have already left on his night off, Nancy realized. Hal wasn't available, either, since he was anchoring the four o'clock news, so she wouldn't be able to tell him about the latest incident.

About an hour later, Ned and Bess arrived in Ned's car, which he parked on the street.

"Nancy, are you all right?" Bess asked anxiously, running up to Nancy's Mustang. Ned didn't say anything. He simply wrapped Nancy tightly in his arms.

"Don't look so worried, you two," Nancy said lightly. "I'm fine—see?" She twirled around for them to see.

"I wish I could say the same for your car," Ned said. He pulled off Nancy's smashed muffler pipe, which had been mangled by the encounter with the truck.

Nancy sighed. "This car saved my life today," she said. "So what if it needs a little repair work."

The three teenagers piled into Ned's car for the

trip to KSM Express. "Are you sure you want to go back there after what happened today?" Bess asked. "Maybe you should just report the incident to the police."

"They can't do much unless I give them something to go on," Nancy pointed out. "I'm looking for evidence that could tie today's assault to the attacks on Hal."

"That bumper seems like pretty strong evidence to me," Bess said. As she closed Ned's passenger door, she glanced uneasily over her shoulder at Nancy's ruined fender.

"Who do you think is behind this attack by the truck?" Ned asked Nancy. Following the directions she gave him, he headed toward KSM Express.

"It had to be someone who overheard my conversation with Hal, then relayed my whereabouts to Milhaus or whoever was driving the truck," Nancy said. "Marilyn is certainly a possibility, or even Gary Krieger. I haven't ruled him out yet. In any case, they must be aware somehow that I have the tape. That's probably why they attacked *me* this time instead of Hal."

They drove east until they reached the commercial-industrial section where KSM Express was located. From a distance, Nancy could see several trucks backed up to the KSM loading dock. The yellow truck with blue pinstriping wasn't among them.

"I want to get behind the warehouse to see if the truck is parked back there," she said.

Ned pointed to a large wire gate that stretched

across the parking lot. "That may be difficult," he said. "The driveway is blocked."

Looking around, Nancy spotted a truck that was stopped on the street in front of KSM Express. It had been left parked with its motor idling.

"The docks in front are all taken up by the other trucks, so maybe they're about to move this truck to the back for the moment," Nancy guessed, thinking out loud. She looked at Ned and Bess. "You two keep an eye out. I'm going to ride the truck in," she said. She hopped out of the car and started walking toward the truck.

"Be careful, Nancy!" Bess called after her.

"Wait, Nancy!" Ned called, running up to her. "Remember what happened last time you sneaked in there. It's too risky!"

But Nancy had already reached the parked truck. The door at the rear of the truck pushed up, like a garage door. With Ned's help, Nancy opened it just enough to wriggle under it. Once her eyes adjusted to the dark interior, she saw that it was loaded with crates of fruit.

Ned looked around, hesitating for a moment. Then he jumped in beside her, pulled down the door so that it was just open a crack, and then settled down between two boxes of pineapples.

"The things I find myself doing when we're together," he said, shaking his head.

They waited quietly for several minutes before they heard the driver return to the truck. The driver unlocked the door to the cab and put the truck into gear. Nancy, Ned, and the pineapples were jostled as the truck lumbered up the driveway to KSM Express.

"Ouch! Now I know how you get to be a bruised banana," Ned joked, keeping his voice low.

A moment later the truck ground to a halt as the driver waited for a couple of workers to swing open the wire gate that blocked off the rear section of KSM. The truck started up again, and Nancy felt herself sway as they rounded a corner. Then the engine was switched off.

Evidently no one was in a hurry to offload the fruit crates, because Nancy and Ned heard the driver and workers' voices fade away as they left for another part of the warehouse.

Nancy peeked under the door and cautiously looked around, then she and Ned slowly raised it and jumped down to the ground. At first she couldn't see anything resembling the truck that had tried to run her down earlier that afternoon. The sun was beginning to go down as she and Ned poked around a stand of trees and bushes at the rear of the lot. There, tucked behind the KSM warehouse, was the pin-striped truck!

"That's it!" she whispered excitedly.

Ned took a deep breath. "Great. Now we're positive we're in total danger," he said nervously.

Nancy looked around to make sure that none of the workers inside the warehouse could see them watching. Then she darted to the far side of the pin-striped truck, followed by Ned. She pulled out her lock-picking tools and quickly got the truck's door open.

"Do we really need to do this?" Ned asked. "Just the truck's being here proves that Kurt Milhaus is tied to these attacks."

"I just want to check it out," Nancy said. She searched the truck's compartments and ran her hands under the seats. "The truck looks pretty clean, though. We may not find anything—"

She paused as her hand hit something behind the seat cushion. "Hmm, what's this?"

Nancy pulled out a faded pamphlet that had been wedged between the seats. It was an old brochure for KLM Express, with a picture of Kurt Milhaus on the cover. Using her penlight, Nancy peered at the caption that ran under Milhaus's picture. She blinked and read the caption a second time.

"Look at this, Ned," she whispered urgently. "The name under Milhaus's picture is Kurt *Steghorn* Milhaus. I think he must be related to Bill Steghorn—the Channel Nine engineer!"

Chapter

Fifteen

NED WAS LOOKING at her as if she were speaking Swahili.

"The *S* in KSM Express stands for Steghorn," Nancy explained. "Now I realize why Milhaus looks so familiar to me—he and Bill Steghorn both have the same kind of bushy eyebrows and heavy features. They must be related. Maybe they're even father and son."

Nancy shook her head. "I *knew* there was something about Milhaus I should have recognized. He must have given Steghorn the trick pen. Then Steghorn accidentally dropped it in the feed booth when he planted the threatening tape."

"If they're father and son, then why would Steghorn and Milhaus have different last names?" Ned asked.

"Steghorn could have divorced Milhaus's mother when he was very young," Nancy said, working it out in her mind. "And Milhaus could have taken his stepfather's last name—that's not so uncommon."

Nancy stuffed the brochure into her pocket. "I've got to show this to Hal Taylor and Otto Liski. As engineer, Steghorn could easily have rigged the live-wire booby trap that almost killed Hal. And it would have been easy for him to create the threatening tape." She frowned, then added, "I still need more proof of Steghorn's involvement in the attacks, though. Something that will stand up in court."

Ned had been looking around the gated parking area while Nancy spoke. "That leaves us with just one problem—how do we get out of here?" he asked. "They're not exactly going to throw us a bon voyage party when we try to get past the gate."

Nancy sneaked a peek through the truck's window. In the distance, she could see two of Milhaus's workers leaning against the locked gate. Glancing around the truck's cab, she spotted a pair of mirrored sunglasses and a baseball cap that was imprinted with the KSM logo. "Ned, do you think you could drive this truck?" she asked.

"I think so," he said. "I drove one of those big

133

rental trucks last summer when I was moving some stuff for my parents. I could probably fake it. What do you have in mind?"

Nancy handed him the hat and sunglasses. "Put these on," she said. She stifled a giggle as he obeyed. "Ned, you really *do* look like a truck driver," she said. "Now you'll have to play the part to get us out of here."

She quickly described her plan to Ned. "We'll drive this truck right out of here—just long enough to make our getaway," she said. "When we get to the gate, just tell the workers that Merrick wants you to move the truck. He's that crazy foreman I told you about who attacked Bess and me. I don't think they'll question an order from him."

"Okay," Ned said, climbing into the driver's seat. Nancy hunched down onto the floor so that she couldn't be seen from the ground. "Here goes," he said, turning the key in the ignition.

The truck's engine roared to life, but it drew little attention from the workers standing by the gate. They were obviously used to the sound of trucks coming and going.

"So far, so good," Ned announced. He shifted the truck smoothly into gear, then drove it up to the gate.

"You new?" Nancy heard a deep voice ask. The man didn't sound very interested.

When Ned nodded, a second voice asked, "Why you headin' out without a load?"

Ned shrugged. "Merrick says move the truck, so I gotta move the truck," he replied.

The men chuckled, and Nancy heard them unlock the gate. "That Merrick'll drive you nuts with all his goofball orders," the first, deep voice said.

A moment later Ned waved his hands and drove through the gate. "Whew!" he exclaimed as they rounded the corner. "That was too easy."

Nancy scrambled up into her seat. "Great, Ned!" she cried. "You should win the Academy Award for that one." She glanced behind the truck as Ned pulled slowly away from KSM Express, but the two men had already forgotten about them.

As soon as they were out of view of the KSM workers, Nancy and Ned turned onto the street where Ned had left his car. Bess was waiting behind the steering wheel, her expression anxious.

"Let's go!" Nancy said to Ned as she opened the door of the truck. They jumped out of the truck and dashed back to Ned's car.

"Thank goodness it's you two," Bess said, giving a sigh of relief. She scooted over to let them in on the driver's side. "I thought that truck had swallowed you up and was coming back to finish me off!"

Ned glanced back at the truck. "Boy, will they be mad when they find that truck is missing from the parking lot," he said.

"What happened back there, anyway?" Bess asked.

"I think I've found our culprit. It's Bill Steghorn, the engineer. I'll have to fill you in on the details later," Nancy said. "Right now I need you to drop me off at my car so I can head back to the station."

Ned shot Nancy a warning glance. "Do you think that's wise? We already know Steghorn could be dangerous," he started to protest, but Nancy overruled him with a firm shake of her head.

"I have to wrap this up before Steghorn really hurts Hal," she said. "I know Steghorn's involved, but I need more proof. I promise to be careful."

"All right," Ned agreed reluctantly. "But I'll be waiting by the phone for you to tell me what happens."

Fifteen minutes later Ned and Bess dropped Nancy off at the service station where she had left her car. She drove quickly back across town to the TV station. By the time she reached the newsroom, the evening news was just ending. She was surprised to see that another reporter, not Hal Taylor, was anchoring the news with Marilyn Morgan.

"Where's Hal?" Nancy asked Marcus Snipes, who was delivering a stack of tapes to an editor.

Marcus shrugged. "Someone said he took the night off. I don't know where he went," he replied. "It's been sort of quiet around here tonight. I haven't seen Otto Liski since early this afternoon, either."

Nancy thanked him and continued down the hallway. She went to the control room and checked the engineering schedule. Steghorn wasn't supposed to be at work that night, she was relieved to note.

Before heading back to the newsroom, Nancy ducked into an empty office and called both Otto Liski and Hal at home. Neither man answered, so she left urgent messages on both their answering machines, asking them to call her back at the station.

For the next several hours, Nancy hid out in an editing booth, pretending to be working on a news assignment. What she was really doing was waiting for the staff to clear out so that she could look for more evidence about Steghorn's involvement in the threats against Hal.

As soon as the late-night news broadcast was finished, most of the remaining reporters and production people left. At midnight, Nancy emerged from the editing booth.

She walked down the long hallway to the front lobby. Everyone was gone except for the night security guard. He sat with his feet up on the reception desk, reading the sports section of the River Heights *Enquirer*. The guard glanced up from his newspaper when he saw Nancy. "Working late tonight?" he asked.

"Yes," Nancy said. "I have some work to catch up on, and I just wanted you to know I was back there."

"Well, don't work too hard," the guard said, and returned to his newspaper.

Nancy's steps echoed in the dim hallways as

she made her way to the back, to Steghorn's locker. The empty corridors had a spooky feel to them in the middle of the night, and Nancy had to go down several of them before she came upon Steghorn's locker. She glanced around quickly just to make sure no one was around. Then she jimmied the padlock.

Inside Steghorn's locker, Nancy was again struck by all the photographs of Marilyn Morgan. On the floor, she found another KSM Express pen. "That clinches the fact that he's connected to Kurt Milhaus," she muttered to herself.

Tucked in the back of the locker she found a small squirt can of lighter fluid. Nancy picked up the can and shook it. It was half-empty.

"Steghorn must have used this to start the fire in Hal's office," she mused.

The last item that caught her eye in the locker was a minicassette recorder. It was sitting in the bottom of Steghorn's locker next to a box of tapes. The tapes were organized by dates, Nancy saw.

She popped the most recent tape into the recorder—and was stunned to hear her own voice discussing the case with Hal Taylor. The conversation was the one she'd had over the phone with Hal Taylor earlier that day, Nancy realized with a start.

"He's been wiretapping the phones at the station!" she exclaimed softly. That was why the attacker seemed to know her every move!

"That's right, Nancy," a deep voice spoke up

just behind her. "Too bad you had to find out about it."

Nancy whirled around, letting the tape recorder drop into her jacket pocket. Bill Steghorn was standing just a few feet away from her. He was holding a gun, and it was pointed straight at her!

Chapter

Sixteen

Nancy took a deep breath, trying not to focus on the gleaming metal gun barrel. But the cold glimmer in Bill Steghorn's eyes was an equally sinister sight.

"Such a lovely young girl," the engineer said slowly. "Too bad you had to get yourself mixed up in all of this."

"By 'all of this' I assume you mean your attacks on Hal Taylor?" Nancy asked. She wanted to get as much information as possible out of Steghorn while she stalled for time.

"Exactly," the engineer said. "You have to understand, Nancy. I'm just a father trying to protect his son from having his reputation smeared on network television."

"So you *are* Kurt Milhaus's father—and you've been trying to scare Hal Taylor into dropping his story on your son's bribery payments to Steve Gilbert," Nancy said. While she was talking, she surreptitiously turned on the minicassette recorder that was in her pocket. Everything they said was now being recorded.

"How did you find out about Hal's story in the first place?" she asked.

Bill Steghorn shrugged. "There aren't many secrets in a news station," he said. "Besides, Hal's habit of farming out all his work meant that at least a dozen people knew about the story he was working on—including me."

The engineer advanced on Nancy, keeping the gun aimed at her heart. "At first I thought I could scare him away from the story," he explained. "That's why I sent the warning letters and the tape. When that didn't work, I set the fire in his office and stole the incriminating tape."

Steghorn took a deep breath and continued. "But Hal still didn't back off, so I knew I'd have to get rid of him—permanently. My son is the only good thing I have in my life. Besides," he added, his nostrils flaring, "if you knew how Hal mistreated Marilyn . . . I was taping his conversations, so I know how he upset her when he broke their engagement. She deserves better than that. That's when I realized he had to die."

Nancy couldn't believe how cold and callous Steghorn sounded. "How does Clay Jurgenson fit into the attacks?" she pressed. "Has he been helping you?"

141

"Clay Jurgenson is a free-lance extortionist," Steghorn said. "He caught me setting the electric wire trap for Hal in the newsroom ceiling, and he threatened to go to Otto Liski unless I paid him twenty-five thousand dollars."

"So you set up a meeting between him and your son to make the payoff," Nancy guessed.

Steghorn looked surprised. "So you found out about that," he said. "You're a good detective, Nancy. Too good. That's why you'll have to die, I'm afraid."

Nancy felt a surge of fear at the threat. She hoped that the security guard would make his rounds this way soon. She didn't see any way to make a move with that gun on her.

Bill Steghorn seemed to sense her thoughts. "Unfortunately, you won't be able to escape like you did earlier today," he said. "That was some fancy driving you did, though, I have to admit."

Nancy drew in a sharp breath. "So it was you driving that truck," she said.

Steghorn shook his head. "Merrick was doing the actual driving. I was the one who searched Hal's house. I had to take off when you arrived with your friend, but I waited around the corner for you to leave. Then I followed you and relayed your movements to Merrick on my cellular car phone. He caught up with you as soon as you started climbing that hill."

Nancy glanced again at the photographs of Marilyn Morgan. "And you also tore all the pictures of Hal and Marilyn in half," she said.

"Yes, that was an indulgence on my part," he

said. "With Hal out of the way, maybe Marilyn and I, you know . . ." Steghorn's voice trailed off.

His bushy eyebrows drew together suddenly, giving his face a fierce, determined look. He waved the gun at Nancy. "No more time for talking, I'm afraid. It's time that we departed for our final destination."

Steghorn jabbed the gun against Nancy's neck, forcing her to walk ahead of him toward a rear exit doorway that Nancy hadn't seen before.

"And what exactly *is* our final destination?" she asked, trying to stay calm.

"For you, the final destination is death, I'm afraid," Steghorn said in a tone that made Nancy's blood run cold.

He threw open the exit door, which led to one of the outer parking lots. Nancy felt a rush of cold night air. Just beyond the doorway she could see a panel truck. The back of the truck was open.

Nancy looked into the truck and did a double take. There, with his hands tied together, was Hal Taylor!

"We grabbed Hal when he went home to look at the damage you found," Steghorn told Nancy. "Then I forced him to call the station with a convincing excuse for not anchoring the news tonight."

Hal tried to free his hands without success as Steghorn shoved Nancy toward the van. "Nancy, I'm so sorry I got you into this," Hal said to her.

"We're not giving up yet," Nancy told him in a low voice.

"Hurry up and keep quiet," a voice behind her snapped. Kurt Milhaus was impatiently holding the panel truck's door open, waiting for Nancy to get inside.

"You should have listened to me when I told you to steer Hal away from this story," he told her. "Now it's too late."

Nancy had to do something—anything—to keep the truck from pulling away from the station. "Did your foreman deliberately try to run us down that day at KSM Express?" she asked, still trying to stall for time.

Kurt Milhaus snorted with laughter. "Actually, that *was* an accident. Too bad Merrick didn't kill you that day, though—it would have saved me the trouble!"

Bill Steghorn jabbed his gun into Nancy's back again. "Get in the truck," he ordered.

Just then Nancy heard footsteps coming around the corner of the building. It had to be the security guard making his rounds, she realized.

Bill Steghorn's eyes darted nervously around, but before he could do anything, the unsuspecting security guard rounded the corner of the station. His eyes widened with surprise at the sight of the engineer and the gun.

Nancy reacted swiftly. Her leg shot out in a lightning-quick karate kick, knocking the gun out of Steghorn's hand. At the same instant, Hal kicked the panel truck's door open with his feet, knocking over Kurt Milhaus. The motion caused him to roll out of the van and onto the concrete, but Nancy didn't have time to help him.

When Milhaus staggered to his feet, Nancy shoved him into the truck and deftly locked him inside. By this time, the guard had pulled his gun. He was aiming uncertainly at Bill Steghorn.

"What—what's going on?" the guard demanded.

Nancy helped Hal untie his hands, then she turned to face the confused guard. "We'll explain everything to you, *after* we put in a call to the police."

Chapter
Seventeen

I CAN'T BELIEVE I'm finally getting to meet Hal Taylor," Bess said as she walked with Nancy into the Channel 9 lobby the following afternoon. Several people were decorating the lobby with garlands and Christmas decorations. Everyone seemed to be in a festive mood.

The night before, the police had arrived quickly to round up Bill Steghorn and Kurt Milhaus. They had arrested Steve Gilbert and Clay Jurgenson at their homes soon after.

Now that the case was solved, Nancy was ready to relax and enjoy the Christmas holiday. Unfortunately, Ned had returned to Emerson that morning for his final exams, but he would be back before Christmas.

Nancy grinned at Bess. "I'm afraid your timing's pretty lousy with Hal, Bess," she said. "It looks like he and Marilyn may get back together."

As if to confirm her words, Hal walked into the lobby and over to Marilyn, who was hanging an ornament on the tree.

"Let's forget our breakup ever happened," Nancy heard Hal saying to Marilyn. Marilyn responded by circling Hal's neck in a gentle embrace. Then Hal looked up and spotted Nancy standing nearby.

"Nancy!" he called waving to her. He was holding up a videotape. "After the police came last night I stayed up until all hours recutting the bribery story. This one could win me an award—a powerful local corruption story with a socko ending—Milhaus, Steghorn, Gilbert, and Jurgenson in jail! It's going to air tonight instead of Monday."

"I'm glad it worked out, Hal," Nancy said as she and Bess joined the co-anchors. "Hal, Marilyn, I'd like you to meet my friend Bess Marvin."

"I really admire your work, Hal," Bess said enthusiastically.

"Well, thank you very much," Hal said, turning his famous smile on her.

Marilyn tugged at Hal's sleeve. "Remember, it's time for your interview, Hal," she said.

Hal leaned over and whispered in Nancy's ear. "I think Marilyn and I are back on track," he said. "Nearly getting killed last night made me rethink my priorities in a big way—especially where Marilyn is concerned."

For the first time since they'd met each other, Marilyn smiled at Nancy. "Hal told me everything you did to track down the attacker. I can't believe Bill Steghorn was behind it all along," she said. "During the past few months I thought of him as a friend, but now I realize my mistake." She shuddered. "Whoever would have thought he was such a creep!"

"You could clear up one thing for me, Marilyn," Nancy said. "Why did you have that meeting with Steve Gilbert last week?"

Marilyn looked sheepishly from Nancy to Hal. "I never kept that meeting," she said. "I got so crazy with jealousy that I was thinking of trying to scoop Hal on his own story. But at the last minute I couldn't go through with it." She gently cupped Hal's chin with her hand. "From now on, we'll concentrate on supporting each other's work, not competing."

"Everything should go back to normal around here now," Hal added. "Marilyn's decided to stay at the station, and we've made a pact to help each other professionally."

Nancy felt a tap on her shoulder, and she turned to see Otto Liski standing there.

"I heard I missed all the excitement yesterday," he said. "See what happens when the producer takes a night off once a year?" he joked. Liski gave her a hug. "Anyway, we all owe you a lot of thanks, Nancy," he said. "You've got a great career waiting for you in television, if you ever want it."

Standing behind him was Gary Krieger. "Don't encourage her, Liski—I don't need the competition!" he joked. "Seriously, Nancy, you'd make a great reporter."

Nancy smiled at the two men. "Thanks, but I'll stick with detective work for now," she said.

"Nancy!"

Nancy turned at the sound of the familiar, grating voice. It was Brenda Carlton. Notebook in hand, she was staring at Hal Taylor.

"I promised you your exclusive interview, Brenda, and here he is," Nancy said. "Hal will fill you in with all the details about Gilbert's arrest."

Nancy had barely introduced Brenda to Hal and Marilyn, when the reporter elbowed her aside. "I understand you helped capture Bill Steghorn and the others," Brenda said to Hal.

"Nancy's the one who really saved the day—and my life—" Hal began, but Brenda interrupted him.

"Oh, but, Hal, I'd much rather hear about *you*," she gushed. "Tell me all about the experience you've just been through."

Nancy caught Bess's eye. The two of them smiled knowingly as they listened to Brenda's interview. Brenda was definitely up to her old tricks again. It was clear that Hal Taylor, not Nancy Drew, would be the hero in tomorrow's newspaper!

Nancy linked arms with Bess, and the two friends walked out together into the bright winter sunlight.

Nancy's next case:

There's something funny going on down at the hot new comedy club Over the Rainbow—and someone's laughing all the way to the bank. The club's accountant has been sent to jail for embezzlement, and Nancy is convinced he's been framed. She's gone undercover at the Rainbow, determined to catch the real crook's act.

But the pot of gold at the end of this Rainbow is buried in deceit and dirty tricks. Nancy suspects that the club is a front for an illegal gambling operation and that she faces the toughest kind of crowd. Not only are the stakes dangerously high, but the players in the game have a very nasty sense of humor . . . in *NO LAUGHING MATTER,* Case #79 in the Nancy Drew Files™.